Finding a dead man is a hell of a way to start a holiday.

Growing up, Hawk was always a bit of a wild card. Once he became a SEAL, he found his niche in the world. But the wild man was still there, under wraps ...and waiting for a match. Back home for a few days, he realizes a new, darker element has moved in.

And it appears to involve the freckle-faced redhead he never forgot.

Mia remembers her best friend's brother. After all, what woman could forget him? He was like fireworks lighting up her life. Taking her breath away and making her heart beat faster. But the version that came home was harder, more dangerous ... and sexy as hell.

Good thing he's on their side as the town explodes in violence with Mia caught in the middle.

Books in This Series:

HAWK

SEALs of Honor, Book 2

Dale Mayer

HAWK: SEALS OF HONOR, BOOK 2
Dale Mayer
Valley Publishing

Copyright © 2016

ISBN-13: 978-1-928122-77-7

Praise for Dale Mayer

I love to read Dale Mayer's books... keeps me guessing.... I am getting good though trying to figure out who did it.... I am on my fourth book....

...Review left on Vampire in Deceit, book 4 of Family Blood Ties

Dale Mayer's work is always outstanding and Haunted by Death is no exception.

...Review from Haunted by Death, book 2 of the By Death Series

This is a GREAT series that you don't want to miss out on!

...Review from Broken Protocols Series

This is my favorite author I enjoy all her books and I can't wait for more... her books are easy to get into and I love the storyline

...Review from Dangerous Designs, book 1 of the Design Series

Dale Mayer is a gifted writer who now has me hooked as a new fan. She characters are complex and she shares her knowledge of energy work clearly and simply. Makes for fascinating reading...

...Review from Rare Find, book 6 of Psychic Visions Series

Don't underestimated Dale Mayer. Combination of JD Robb and Heather Graham. Paranormal suspense.........

...Review left on Maddy's Floor, book 3 of the Psychic Visions Series

Wow! I read a lot, and I can honestly say that there a few books that I have read that I will remember for years. This is one of those books. Thank you Dale for giving me the gift of this magnificent story. It was both heartbreaking and hopeful at the same time.

...Review left on Skin, book 1 of Broken and yet...Healing Series

Touched by Death is an outstanding novel by Dale Mayer. Unlike her usual novels that contain paranormal activity, this novel is sheer malevolent actions from ordinary humans.

...Review left on Touched by Death, book 1 of By Death Series

Dale's books are spellbinding in more ways than one. She has a unique way with words. Her characters are fun and funny and loving. I love the way the story flows. Her characters all have personality. She takes you from suspense to love, then fear love and eternal love.

...Review left on Second Chances, book 1 of Second Chances... at Love Series

CHAPTER 1

H AWK LORING STARED at the commotion boiling over on the corner of the street. Having just driven into his hometown to visit with his sister, he had no idea what happened, but the place was a mess. People ran from one side of the road to the other. Small groups forming, then reforming as new people joined. What the hell was going on?

Someone raced in front of him. He hit the brakes hard. His town had changed if people were aiming for suicide by car.

Canford used to be the calmest, most laid back of all small towns in the US.

He pulled his Jeep up in front of the general store he'd worked at as a kid, slightly surprised to see it was still there. Gordon, the owner, was aging. He'd threatened to sell out many times. But as business was booming with the caving and hiking groups, and the new summer condo units going up on the nearby lake, he'd obviously held off making a decision.

Of course Canford catered to the caving enthusiasts during the summer and hunters during the winter, giving his business more year round stability.

Shoving his sunglasses into place he hopped out, gave a narrow look at the people still running around, a worried expression on their faces. His penetrating gaze went from one to the other and saw the same hunched shoulders, frowns and looks over their shoulders, heard the rapid voices and excitable speech patterns. He watched as two groups melded into one.

Senses alert and curiosity piqued, he headed into the store to get the details. Nothing ever happened around town Gordon didn't know about. Hawk doubted that had changed.

The store was cool, shadowed, and after a long glance around, empty.

"Gordon?" No answer. The storefront was empty and no one stood at the cash counter.

He walked to the back office where the man could always be found. Sure enough he was there now too – facedown on the floor with a nice neat round hole in the back of his head.

What the hell had gone on here?

Hawk crouched and checked out the body. Still warm but cooling. Dead a few hours at least. Did anyone know? Had anyone come in and checked on him? Anger boiled up. Gordon was a good man. Helped out anyone and everyone. He didn't deserve to be shot in the back. Hell, no one did.

Was that what the town was agog about?

And where the hell was the sheriff? Someone should be leading the investigation.

He stared down at his old friend, hating to see him this way. He couldn't see much of the face and there was less hair than he remembered. Then again, Gordon had been going bald for years so he shouldn't be surprised.

As he tamped his anger down, his phone went off. Swede checking in. The team had five days off, and each headed off somewhere. Swede was going home. Mason was going to the beach with Tesla to help her heal from the ordeal she'd been through. This last job had taken them to places they hadn't expected to go. With his free time, Hawk had decided family was just the ticket. That meant his sister. There was no one else. And she was good people. Reminded him a lot of Tesla.

Tesla…if she had a sister, he'd have been all over her. As it was, Mason had struck gold, and even if it took him awhile, he had finally understood she was a gift worth keeping.

After seeing something he'd had no idea even existed, Hawk wanted the same for himself.

But how did one go about finding it – or her – in this case? Women like Tesla were rare.

Swede's text said he'd made it back to his father's house safe and sound and where the hell was Mason? Wanting to avoid the multiple texts required to explain, Hawk quickly dialed his friend and fellow SEAL.

"I'm in Canford. Stopped in town to say hi to Gordon," Hawk said, glad Swede knew the town and Gordon after multiple visits to the hunting cabin for R&R, and quickly filled him in on what he'd found.

"What? Gordon? Just lying there? Shit." Banked anger seeped through the phone. "Give me a few hours and I'll be there."

Hawk didn't have a chance to argue because the phone went dead. Knowing Swede, he'd already hugged his father good-bye and thrown his kit into his truck and was even now hitting the road. They were about four hours apart. Not that he needed him, but that was what mates did.

Then he remembered his sister, Eva.

And winced.

She'd been fairly voluble on her opinion of Swede. An unfortunate beginning had given her a bad impression of the behemoth. Maybe this time that could be changed.

Not likely. His sister was a spitfire and not into multiple affairs at the same time, and there was something about Swede's looks and size that had women all over him. Hell, they were SEALs, women were *never* in short supply. There were bars close to the base that appeared to cater to women who only wanted to catch a SEAL. Then a different one the next night and on and on. Like Mason, Hawk had gotten tired of the whole singles game, and now that he knew there was something else out there – hell, sign him up!

Mason was a lucky man.

He turned his attention back to the floor. Gordon's body lay half hidden by the desk, but anyone could come in and see him. Hawk grabbed a blanket out of the cupboard and covered him up. He had no idea where Gordon's only daughter Mia was, but he didn't want her to come in and see her father like this.

He called in the local police department or what passed for one here. There'd been a sheriff and a couple of deputies the last time he'd been through. He brought up his phone again to call his sister when the main entrance burst open and two men ran in. Hawk stepped out of the office to face two young bucks.

They skittered to a stop and glared at him. "Who the fuck are you?"

His eyebrows shot up and his gaze narrowed, memorizing their faces, making sure he'd recognize the two men again.

"Maybe I should be asking you that question?" he said in a hard voice. "And what are you doing here?"

The first one reared back slightly, his long hair billowing over his forehead, a smirk on his face. "It's a store, what do you think we're doing here?"

The second man, a bright redhead covered in freckles, sauntered over to the counter, grabbed a pack of gum and opened it. He tossed a piece to his buddy and took a strip for himself before popping it into his mouth. Then pocketed the rest.

Hawk watched him, anger burning. He'd made no attempt to pay for it. Nor had he even looked to see if Gordon was around. As in he didn't expect him to be here.

Had these two been the killers? He motioned to the gum in the man's pocket. "You gonna pay for that?"

"Na, see it's my store."

Hawk turned his head ever so slightly. The two men backed up.

"Did you say it's your store?" Hawk asked in a low, deadly soft voice.

The long-haired punk looked at the redhead. "Well, it will be. My old man is buying it off of Gordon."

"Then it's not your store right now, is it?" Hawk said, his voice hard.

The two men were smarter than he gave them credit for as the one man pulled out a handful of change and tossed it on the counter. "There. No biggie. Gordon doesn't mind."

They backed up a step.

Hawk advanced. "He doesn't?"

The two men shook their heads. The second one grabbed a chocolate bar off the shelf as he headed for the door. "Nah," he called back defiantly. "He doesn't mind in the least." And the two raced out laughing like loons.

Hawk stood inside the door, looking out the window as he called his sister. "Eva, what the hell is going on?"

There was a weird crackling then her harried voice. "No one really knows, but some rumor started about there being a cache of weapons and bomb making equipment found in one of the caves, and everyone is making up weird conspiracy theories. Where are you?" she asked.

"In the general store, standing over Gordon's dead body." What the hell? Canford and bomb making equipment. Those two didn't go together. Never had. This was country at its finest. Slow, easy, and very quiet.

He heard her cry of horror. "What?"

"He's been shot through the back of the head."

"Oh my God." There was a shocked silence then she said, "Any sign of anyone else around?"

"Half the damn town appears to be standing around," he snapped. "And they look both excited and terrified."

"I know. I am too." There was an odd sound like gears crunching. He looked outside and watched his beau-tiful sister get out of her ancient truck and run up the stairs to the front door, her cell phone still at her ear.

She burst through the door.

And ran into his arms.

He held her close, her long auburn hair hanging down her back and over his arms. He wrapped a hand in her long locks and hugged her hard. Finally he set her back a few feet and saw the worry in her face. He gave her a little shake.

"A cache of weapons?"

"And bomb making equipment and…" she took a deep rag-ged breath. "Chemicals. And many of the tubs are empty."

He shook his head. "If that were the case, there'd be the mili-tary here. Hell, I could just as easily be called as well, depending on what's needed."

She nodded. "The sheriff hasn't said anything. The locals are just rehashing gossip, but no one knows anything for sure."

"Then I can guarantee that someone else knows because town gossip never stays local."

"True, but the sheriff was trying to keep everyone calm until he could get the right people here. As in *his* contacts. As far as I know there is a mess of people coming, but in the meantime no one is allowed to leave. And everyone is terrified. No one is drinking the water in case it's poisoned, etc."

He nodded. Rumors ran rampant without any kind of control. But he also understood people. That meant there was going to be hoards of media within hours. Canford was off the beaten track, but there were good roads in and out.

They'd find the small town eventually.

Eva gripped his arms. "Did you mean it…what you said about Gordon?"

He tugged her back into his arms for a quick hug then stepped back and motioned to the office door. "He's behind there."

A fist went to her mouth and tears twinkled at the corner of her eyes. "Who would do such a thing?"

He shrugged. In his world people did all kinds of shitty things for minor reasons. His gaze roamed the back wall, and the question popped out at him. "When were you in the store last?"

She shook her head, her hands swiping at the tears trickling down her cheeks. "A few days ago I think. To see Mia."

Mia. Gordon's daughter. Right, and she was Eva's best friend. "Any idea where she is?"

"Spelunking training," she whispered. "I've been calling her but she's not answering."

Of course not. No reception underground. Spelunking. Really?

"And the gun case over there." He pointed to the empty one on the wall. "Do you remember if it was empty before?"

She gasped and stared. "I have no idea."

He walked over to the cabinet and could see the lock had been smashed. Had Gordon refused to open it? He would. He was that kind of man. He'd also have been damn mad to have his guns taken and used in a criminal offense. Especially in his own murder.

"Do you think it's related?"

"No idea, but how could it not be? When a town goes wild, then the townsfolk do too. Anyone scared and not owning their own firearms might have considered this worth doing to protect themselves. And the theft of the firearms might not have anything to do with Gordon's death. Given where he lay, they may not have seen his body. Or after finding the store deserted they might have just taken the opportunity to snatch the firearms. But chances are the two incidences were related. A stretch not to be."

Then he remembered the earlier visitors.

"Two young punks came in ten minutes before you got here. One planned to steal a pack of gum, and the other one did take a chocolate bar and laughed about it."

"And you didn't pound them into the ground?" she asked in surprise. "Wow, what happened to my big brother?"

"Gordon was lying in the office, and I wanted to find out if they knew. But outside of stealing and acting as if they knew Gordon wouldn't know, they made no actions that let me see they knew anything about his murder."

"Billy and Travis," she said instantly. "Bullies and local rich boys."

"So rich they have to steal?" He saw it often. Rich kids who figured the rules didn't apply to them. Only Canford wasn't a hotspot for the rich. Although the condos on the lake were changing that. If Billy and Travis were examples of the new arrivals he wasn't impressed.

"Something like that. Billy's father is buying up land throughout the area right now." She shrugged. "Lots of people are selling and lots are holding out. Causing a big division in opinion locally."

"The one kid mentioned his father was buying the store from Gordon."

Eva shook her head violently. "No, Gordon was very against that, and he'd been offered a decent price. But he wouldn't have anything to do with it as Tom, the father, planned to give the store to his son, Travis. Mia felt the same way."

"I agree with Gordon." Hawk glanced behind him. "But I wonder how she's going to feel about that now."

CHAPTER 2

M IA DROPPED THE rope she'd wound to a coil by her feet. She'd been doing search and rescue training for months now, but the spelunking was beyond the normal training. She'd been out practicing on her own ever since she'd realized she needed more experience with all the tourist business increasing. The accidents were increasing too. Not a good scenario. More trained personnel were needed.

She searched the gloomy circle of light produced by her headlight. One of the biggest lessons everyone needed to learn was that no one went into the caves alone. Including her. She had both the Bangor brothers with her. And a couple of other search and rescue volunteers all wanting to improve their skills. There was nothing worse than coming up against a lack of training when lives were in jeopardy.

"How is that arm of yours doing, Mia?" Paul asked.

She gave the arm in question a good shake. "It's holding up well." In fact, she was really pleased with it. It had been a good six months since she'd injured it during a bad climb. Months of recovery and therapy and she was back outside as normal. Even so, the arm was a shade weaker than she'd like. Strength was mandatory. During an emergency, weakness was a detriment.

She had to regain the full muscle mass.

"Make sure you don't overdo it, today," Peter warned from behind his brother. "It's easy to do."

"I know." She shook out both arms then grinned. "They feel good."

"Then let's go. This system has some interesting caves further up. Let's get at it."

"I'll lead." She dropped to her knees and crawled through the tunnel, pulling the rope behind her. The others would follow. They'd been down here for a couple of hours already. Time wise they had about another hour then they'd have to turn back. This was the furthest she'd come so it was a success as far as she was concerned.

The return journey should be faster. Good thing. She didn't really enjoy this hobby. And forced herself in here on the premise of work a related skill set. In truth she was a little creeped out being down here in the dark with several tons of dirt ready to come down on her at any moment.

Another reason for being here now. To face that fear.

She'd rather be home to help her friend Eva with the chores. The chores were too much for her on her own. And in truth, Mia enjoyed being around the horses and other animals. She'd been living in the trailer on Eva's property for three months now. A setup that suited both women. Eva needed the cash, and Mia was looking for a place close by but not in her father's house. They only had each other left in family outside of distant or estranged relatives and they were close, but she needed her on space.

A clod of dirt fell down in front of her nose, raising a plume of dust to float up her nostrils. She coughed several times then cleared her throat several more times. She struggled to pull her water bottle forward so she could take a drink. Only it wasn't possible given the confines of the small tunnel. There was nothing else to do but carry on. She crawled forward, still coughing slightly. When she made it through to another cavern, she shifted off to the side, yanked on her rope a couple of times and pulled her water bottle clear. After a long drink, she settled back down against the dirt wall and waited for the others to come along. She'd never been in this section before and knew a lot of this area was full of unchartered caves.

It didn't take long for Peter to poke his head through the whole. He skimmed forward on his stomach. She laughed. "If you gain any more weight, you're going to have trouble getting through to the next cave."

He gave a rustic laugh as he stood up and brushed the dirt off his shirt and pants. "I'm a while off of that fate."

She grinned. "I can just imagine," she said in a mocking voice. "Help 911. There's a rotund man stuck underground. He's caught in the tunnels between the caves. You'll need a large back hoe to rescue him."

"Hey, it's not that bad." And in truth it wasn't, but she loved to tease him. It was almost expected. He'd known her since she was in diapers. He'd been teasing her for just as long.

Paul popped his head through next. "Hey. Are we carrying on again, or is this as far as we're going?"

Peter took a look at his watch. "Time is short. We're going to need to return soon." He pulled out his map and checked the cave chart system. "We have options. There is another exit close to here, but we'd have to walk up hill to the vehicles. There's a lot more territory we'd enjoy covering given the time, maybe that's an idea for next trip. We could enter close by and pick up from here."

"I'm good to do that, but for today, this is probably as far as we can go." She took another long drink of water and surveyed the huge cavern they were in. This was one of the major destinations in the system. It was fascinating if a little scary to be this deep underground.

As the last person made his way through the tunnel, she stood up, checked that everyone was okay and in good health. Then she took a short walk around the cave. Interesting place. There were other tunnels in the system. All headed off in various directions. Fascinating. She could spend days down here and still not explore them all. It would be dead easy to get lost. And that was something she had no intention doing.

There were available maps of the caves that had been charted, but the GPS points were listed with the realization anything electronic was not dependable underground. Although many enthusiasts were trying to shift wholly to digital cave surveying, it was hit or miss at best. And in the dark, shadows lying long in the cavern, she knew how easy it was to get turned around.

And that was often what brought her down here. People who'd lost their way and needed help to get back to the surface. So far, they'd been lucky. No fatalities.

If they were leaving soon, she wanted to take a moment and explore. There was something almost alien about these caves. So huge, so empty, and yet you knew they weren't completely empty when something scurried away into the dark. The air was stale, stagnant yet cool with a mysterious unknown quality to the place. She didn't know what to think of it. She'd been in many caves in the last year, but not like this. Not this deep. Not this far away from the sunlight. In a way it was the sunlight that she missed. The caves themselves to her were like old musty basements. Someplace she needed to go but hated the cramped shadowy spaces that hid more than they revealed.

It was never going to be her hobby.

As long as she learned to do rescues down here for when she was needed to help out, then she was good to not come for pleasure. And based on that...she'd better take a serious look around in case she never returned. She wandered the perimeter of the cave, marveling at the sheer size of the room. Her boots clinked on something metallic. She bent down and found a shell casing. Interesting. Not a good place for shooting practice. She glanced around, but there was no sign of anything having been shot. Still, casings meant people and people meant litter. She slipped it into her pocket. Each of the caves in the system had its own name. She'd forgotten which she was in. They went on and on like a hidden ring of pearls.

There were nooks and crannies that were impossible to see until she was right beside them. There were fallen rocks making the walking treacherous and dirt fell off the roof enough times to remind her they were miles underground with tons of dirt and rock above her head and nothing but more dirt and rock holding it all up.

A freaky thought.

After completing one loop around the cave, noting at least three places where tunnels appeared to head off in different directions she walked slowly back to the others. There was no water in this cave, she'd seen some in others, but as she walked across the dusty center she could see the ground was softer and might get waterlogged during different seasons as groundwater rose.

Who'd like to scramble on their belly through tunnels running with water? Not her.

"I'd like to spend a couple of days down here. It's so quiet. So close to Mother Nature. Like being back in the womb again," Mike said. "Anyone else?"

Mike was part of the local spelunking club and had contributed to the mapping of this cave system. But his comment made her stomach churn.

She shook her head. "Not me."

"We could check out those other exits and see where they go. Spend a weekend camping down here," he added enthusiastically.

She smiled. "Nah, that's your department." He was a nice enough guy, but she had no plans to spend a weekend down here eating dirt. Partly because as nice as he was, she was afraid he was attempting to turn their casual relationship to something more. And that she wasn't into.

He asked a couple of other people. As their responses weren't as negative as Mia's, she was happy to hear he'd likely get a group together of other enthusiasts.

"Time." John stood up. "Let's go everyone."

She led the way back, again, needing to find a level of comfort with having ropes between her feet and her pack dragging against the dirt roof above her head. The sensation of dirt constantly falling on her head. Worse was the fear. Of having it all come down. Of being buried alive. Of never being found. Closing her eyes briefly, she shoved all the self-defeating thoughts to the back of her mind. It was why she was here. Learning. Practicing. So in an emergency when others were filled with those kinds of thoughts, she could help.

Loose dirt fell on her shoulders, pinging off her hard hat.

Lord it was hard to stay calm at times.

She wished she had elbow pads. They were coming up to the even lower section of the tunnel and she had to snake forward on her belly.

The opening to the second cave was up ahead. Grateful, figuring she'd eaten enough dirt for one day, she pulled herself through the last narrow pinch to where she could come upon her knees then crawl the rest of the way. As she stood up, she took several deep breaths. Thank God that part was over.

She was starting to really hate being down here. Out came her water bottle again and she finished the last of it. She had two more bottles in her car but hadn't carried a second with her.

The others were at the entrance behind her. She watched and waited as Paul got to his feet.

"That's quite a trip, isn't it?" He said with a big grin.

"I'm wondering who was so crazy as to crawl into a hole like that in the first place," she muttered. "Especially considering he couldn't see light at the other end."

Jason laughed. "Men have been exploring since time began. It's what they do."

"Yeah, that's why women stayed home with the babies. It was way better than that." She motioned to the small tunnel she'd made it out of.

"You looked to be handling it better this time," Peter said, studying her face. "Was it better?"

She laughed. "It was. But it's never going to be my favorite sport."

"Good enough. It's not for everyone." Mike stood up and stretched his arms high over his head. "For me, it's more about the finding of new spaces. And that often means going into small shitty ones to find the big glorious ones."

"Understood." She watched as the others arrived, mentally counting the numbers to be sure they were all there. An old habit. "Are we ready to head to the vehicles?"

They all nodded. Peter fell into step beside her as they walked through the midsize cavern leading to the first cave in the system and the way back out. She rolled her shoulders and gently massaged her neck.

"How's the arm?"

She smiled. It was a common question these days. "It's all good."

The walk to the sunshine and green woods was easy from that point on. Once outside and a good distance away from the cliff rising behind her, she turned on her phone and checked her messages. And froze.

"Shit."

"I'VE JUST CONTACTED Mia," Eva said. "She'll get the message when she's got cell reception again."

"Did she find the cave with the weapon stash?"

Eva shook her head. "No. She likely doesn't know about it yet."

He nodded. "She will soon." He motioned toward the office where Gordon's body lay. "I've called the sheriff. But no one has shown up yet."

"He's probably thinking anything to do with Gordon's general store is small potatoes compared to what else he might be dealing with. Besides, we're still a law unto ourselves. The sheriff rarely comes here unless we make life really ugly for them."

"So things haven't changed much." Hawk remembered being a little wild growing up in the country where the only thing to do was the single bar at night. But he'd been into hunting, horses and women, even back then. Now he came for the peace and countryside and the sheer *lack* of people. He lived and worked in close confines to the extent his team were brothers. Friends, but more family. They knew each other like he'd never known anyone else, and he found a sense of camaraderie that hadn't been in his life experience up until then. Now he didn't want to do without it – them. They were who he depended on in life. But at night, it was nice to have someone to love, to hold.

He'd met Mia a couple of times but didn't know her. She was his sister's best friend but that relationship had only been close in the years after he'd left. Now he remembered her as a redhead with braces and a face covered in freckles. He had to admit the freckles fascinated him. But she was likely after a stay home kind of guy. So many were.

And he was anything but.

His gaze went to his watch then strayed to the office. Gordon needed to be taken care of. Damn it. Leaving him like that ate at him.

He hadn't seen Gordon much in the last five years, but he'd been a good man. He hadn't deserved this.

"Are you sure it's Gordon?" Mia asked suddenly. "He's not been doing much walking. It doesn't make any sense that would be him." She spun around. "In fact, I haven't seen him for a few months, so I'm not sure how ambulatory he is…"

Her words caught him by surprise. Ambulatory? He spun around to ask her when the sounds of a vehicle screaming into the parking distracted them both. He raced to the window to look out.

A blue Ford, beat up and covered in dust, drove to the front steps and came to a screeching stop.

A tall lean redhead hopped out, a braid swinging down her back. Mia.

CHAPTER 3

MIA BOLTED OUT of her truck, slamming the door in her panic. She jumped the stairs to her father's general store and shoved the door open hard. She ran inside, her heart pounding in fear, a sweaty itch all over her body. Please let the message be wrong. Please let her father be okay. They had their problems but he was all she had. And she so wasn't ready to lose him.

Her wild dash ended against a solid wall of muscle and arms restraining her.

Still panicked, she acted instinctively and brought her arm up, her elbow to his throat, her knee automatically lifting as she twisted.

And just as suddenly she was grabbed, spun and held immobile against a heavily muscled chest, his voice calm and clear as he said, "I'm not going to hurt you. You need to calm down."

She stilled. Then twisted so she could look at his face. And recognized him. Her shoulders sagged. Eva's brother. "Hawk?"

"Yes, it's me. Are you going to stop trying to desex me?"

The arms held her firm. She nodded once. He dropped his arms and stepped back. She still trembled, her mind screaming at her to ask him about her father. A sound burst through from the back office.

Eva.

Eva with tears running down her face at the sight of her friend. Mia shook her head. "Please tell me you were wrong. That he's fine."

Eva shook her head and ran to hug Mia. "I'm so sorry," she whispered. "It looks like it's him."

"No, oh no." Mia burst into tears, her arms tight around Eva. "Please not."

She stared at him, looking for confirmation.

He nodded once.

"Oh." She shoved her fist into her mouth to hold back her cries.

"I found him." Hawk's harsh voice cut through the air. "He's been shot through the head in his office."

She gave a small scream and pivoted to look in the direction of the door. Then slowly approached, she opened the door and stopped at the sight of a blanket shrouded body on the floor. Tears flooding her gaze, she slowly sank beside him, her heart breaking. With a shaking hand she reached out to pull the blanket back. And cried out in shock. "Oh my God. It's not my father."

"What?" Hawk roared.

Hawk and Eva ran to her side.

"No, it's my Uncle Gerry."

"Really? Holy shit." Eva dropped and wrapped her arms around her friend. "It's horrible to think this is a good thing, but…"

"This is a good thing."

"Since when did Gordon have a brother?" Hawk demanded. He squatted beside the body and rolled it over slightly so he could see the face and confirm her words. "Damn, I'm so sorry. I thought this man had a little less hair, but I haven't seen Gordon in quite a while.

"It's okay, you didn't know. They look tons alike." Mia sniffled back her tears, her heart aching with the continuous shocks, but relief was the primary one. "He showed up a few months ago." She wiped her eyes with her sleeve. "They've been estranged for decades."

"And he just showed up out of the blue?"

"Yeah, at first Dad didn't know what to do." She sniffed again and gently lay the blanket back over the body. "Dad is going to be so upset."

"Where is Gordon?" Hawk asked.

"He should be at home. He has been most of the time since the accident. Especially if Gerry was here."

"What accident? And was Gerry working for your father?"

Both Eva and Mia glanced over at him then at each other. Mia groaned. "You don't know."

"Know what?"

"Dad was in a car accident a few months ago. He's in a wheelchair. The doctors say he's going to get better eventually, but right now he's having trouble with mobility, so he's confined to a wheelchair until he's stronger."

Hawk's gaze searched her face then dropped to the body on the floor.

"I wonder if the bullet was meant for your father or your uncle?"

She stared at him and shook her head. She pulled out her phone and called her father, her gaze on her uncle, her heart not sure how to react after the shock, the relief and now back to panic. The phone was picked up and before anyone could answer, she jumped in with, "Dad, you there?"

"I'm here," he answered. "How was the caving?"

She closed her eyes, tears collecting in the corners as his warm caring voice filled her ears and her heart. "It was okay. But there's something I have to tell you."

"Oh, what's that?"

"It's Uncle Gerry. He's been shot."

She heard her father suck in his breath hard. Then a half cough. "What? How? Are you sure?"

"He's been shot in the head."

"Damn it. Where?" His voice fumed in a mixture of pain and anger.

"I'm in your office staring down at him now. Eva's brother Hawk, found him."

"Hawk's in town?" His voice regained some strength as he registered Hawk's name.

"Yes, he's called the authorities but they haven't arrived yet." No surprise there.

"Apparently a cache of weapons was found in one of the caves." Her father muttered. "Gerry mentioned something about bombs and chemicals this morning when I talked to him."

"After the ambulance comes to collect him, I'll take you down to the hospital so you can see him."

"Yeah." He cleared his throat. "I'd appreciate that."

Hearing the roughness in his voice, she felt her own tears burn her eyes all over again as she said good-bye. She turned to the others staring at her and shrugged. "He needs to say good-bye."

Hawk nodded once. She turned her back on him and clasped

her hands around her knees and rocked in place. With Eva's arm wrapped around her, she sat in silence.

Unlike Hawk. Who paced.

Mia looked over at Eva. "How long has he been here?"

"He got into town just an hour ago. I was expecting him today, just not when."

"He's on days off?"

"Yeah." Mia grinned. "Five days."

"Nice." She studied him covertly. She'd heard about the arrogant, so damn sexy SEALs.

She had nothing against men. Even loved a few. But some were just more than others.

Hawk was one of those.

More. Everything. More presence. More male. More power.

But he was a SEAL. The ultimate of warriors. So not for her.

She'd never felt like she was enough. Could ever be enough. So she'd never entered the race. Why would she? She hated to fail and it was a given she'd fail that one.

IT *WASN'T* GORDON. Shit. How could he have made that mistake? Hawk had to take another look. See what he'd missed. Moving the women to the other side, Hawk crouched down, pulled the blanket back and studied the dead man's features.

Mia spoke behind him. "They've got an uncanny resemblance. Maybe because they were Irish twins."

Glancing at her, he realized she was sitting with her back to the body. She didn't have to see it.

He frowned, trying to dredge up an explanation for that phrase. "Irish twins." Then got it. Both boys had been born in the same year. And according to what he was seeing, they both looked close enough alike to be real twins.

Speaking of brothers…

Swede. He quickly texted Swede and let him know about the mix up.

His phone rang only minutes after he'd sent it.

"What the hell is going on there, buddy?" Swede sounded exasperated and worried at the same time.

"Damned if I know. Apparently Gordon had a bad accident, and his brother came back into his life after decades of not being there. And now six weeks later he's dead, sporting a bullet that might have been meant for him or for Gordon, and on top of that, apparently someone locally found a cache of guns, bomb making equip-ment and possibly chemical weapons. I don't know where or why or how. And damn it, so far I haven't been able to get any authorities to come to the crime scene or investigate because of it. All units are supposedly involved with finding and cataloging the weapons' cache and tracking down the owner." His frustration ate at him. "Apparently, a murder is a secondary priority."

Swede swore heavily and in several languages. The man was well read and proficient in four. "I'm still coming. So are the others. It's not official, obviously, but some shit is going on."

"I know. There's something else." With an arm motion he caught Mia's attention and motioned to the wall and the gun case. When the color leached from her face, he knew things were going to get worse. "Swede, Gordon's stock of guns has been stolen as well. I need to talk to him. Get a full list."

Swede groaned. "Well, you never could make it easy, could you?"

Hawk snorted. "Not me. I came here for some R&R. A real holiday. Some family time."

"Well, it looks like you found it, SEAL style." And he rang off. So damn true.

Good mood restored, Hawk put his phone away to see Mia hunched over as if in pain.

He ran to her side. "Are you okay?"

She nodded and gamely tried to straighten. "It's just too much," she whispered. "I've heard very little about the weapons' cache." She shook her head. "But what I have heard is not good. And now that Dad's guns have been stolen, well it just adds to the whole mess."

"Have you got any idea *whose* weapons' cache they found?"

"No. It wasn't too far away from where I was today. I've been in the general area before as we all have, yet none of us could have imagined such a stash."

"Did you say chemical weapons, too?" Eva asked in a small voice. "Why?"

He didn't answer. There was no good answer. Weapons like that could be an end of the world type of preparation, someone wanting to have weapons against the alien invasion or worse, terrorists planning an attack on American soil.

And from the look on the women's faces, he suspected that they understood the dangers themselves.

A vehicle drove into the parking lot. He straightened and peered out the window. Finally the damn sheriff.

Hawk walked out to meet him.

"Well, if it isn't our little SEAL guy all grown up."

As a teenager he'd had one goal in life, that was to join the Navy and become a SEAL. He'd faced plenty of mockery then too. That he'd made it wouldn't give him kudos here. Too many were living out broken dreams and didn't want to know of those who reached theirs.

Whatever.

He knew who he was. It might have taken him some time, but he'd gotten there.

Mia stepped forward. "Sheriff McKay."

He spat out a wad of chew off to the side. Good thing. Hawk would have gotten in his face if that had been in Mia's direction. Hawk had no patience for those with a lack of respect.

Mia however appeared to have no idea she was supposed to be treated better.

"My uncle has been murdered," she said in a controlled tone.

"I suggest you let us make that kind of determination," the sheriff said, shifting his belt more comfortably around his hips. "We're the law here."

His gaze sharpened, locked on Hawk's face. "You staying?"

"For a while." But he refused to say more. In fact, he was about to contact his commander and fill him in on the situation. Someone needed to – this guy didn't look like he gave a shit.

CHAPTER 4

N OW WITH THE sheriff there, Mia felt free to leave. She drove home to her father's house. About halfway there, she remembered the shell casing she'd seen in the cave. Were the two incidences related? She should have taken a better look while there. Only hadn't thought at the time it was something to be worried about. She hadn't even said anything about it to the others. Would it have made a difference if she had? She didn't know.

What the heck was going on? The fact that her father's guns were all missing worried her more. Dad kept the other firearms and ammunition at his home. She'd mentioned that to the sheriff and he'd had a fit over it. The sheriff sent a deputy to her father to question him about them. Hell, as if the whole country didn't keep their own stash. Her father just kept more than most. But all his paperwork was in order.

And if the deputy had gone as instructed, where was his vehicle? He should be there by now. She parked and walked up to the front door of the big old log cabin. It had been in the family for generations. "Dad?"

Silence. She pushed open the front door. "Dad, you in here?" No answer. "Dad, where are you?"

Racing through the house, she checked all the rooms. There

was no sign of him.

She pulled out her phone.

"Eva, he's not here."

She listened to her friend's shocked exclamation. "Where could he be?"

"I have no idea." She walked around the perimeter of the house. There were multiple outbuildings and six months ago he'd have been in any one of them. But now in his condition…not likely. All the doors were closed so far.

"Any sign of him."

"No." And she was scared. Like really scared. "Eva?"

"Yeah, what's going on?"

"The other guns are missing."

"From where?"

Mia stood outside her father's locked and guarded storehouse. All stock from the store came here until needed. Always. And the double doors were open, the lights off. But even she could see the empty gun cabinet.

"This is really bad news," she said quietly. She heard a noise behind her.

"Hang on, we're coming there," Eva cried. "Ten minutes."

"It's too late," Mia said softly, her heart halting at the stranger in front of her only to race ahead again at the gun barrel pointed right at her.

"I'm already captured."

"Get off the damn phone. And get over behind your father." The stranger motioned to the back of the building. She couldn't see anything. "How the hell am I going to get him down the damn mountain if he can't walk?"

"He's been in a bad accident," she said, her voice cracking as she walked slowly in the direction he pointed. Please let her father be okay. "He can't walk very far."

"Well, he'd better be able to or else. I'm going to just have to pop him one too. I won't leave any witnesses behind." The gun barrel lifted. "Now get your ass over there."

She swallowed hard and took several more steps closer. As her eyes adjusted to the shadows, she could see the gunman, his face in the shadows still, a pistol in one hand and a rifle under his other arm. Shit. She quickly pocketed her phone. But as she slipped it away, she clicked on the speaker button so Eva could still hear the conversation. In a cool voice, she asked, "Where's my father?"

"Oh he's there. Now move or I'll gun you down where you stand." He gave a shrug. "Don't matter to me."

"What do you want?"

"My cache back."

Double shit. This was the madman with the cave full of weapons.

"I need them."

"What does that have to do with my father?"

"Your father has more weapons." The gunman laughed. "And I've got orders to fill. Weapons to make. If they aren't completed then people are going to be mighty unhappy with me. I can't have that."

"You're making weapons for other people?" she asked in horror. "What kind of weapons?"

"Weapons that will blow a hole in the Empire State Building for one." And he laughed. "You really want a bullet where you're standing, don't you?"

Inside, she suddenly remembered who the first person Eva

would tell of her predicament. Hawk. The SEAL. Feeling better, she smiled at the gunmen, smirking inside as his gaze narrowed. Then she caught sight of her father, lying in a crumpled heap behind him.

"Dad." She raced toward him. "I hope you rot in hell for this," she called behind her.

"Ha, that's a guarantee," he said. "Besides, he wouldn't tell me where the other guns and the ammunition I need for the weapons from the store are."

"How did you know he had any here?"

"Easy, his shifty brother was supposed to get them for me before. But he welshed on his deal. Typical. Never did trust him."

She didn't know what to think. Gerry had betrayed her father. From the look on her father's face, his eyes open and pained, that was exactly what had happened. Damn him to hell after all.

So much for wanting a reconciliation with his brother.

Gerry had come to steal from him. And had ended up dead.

HAWK STARED AT his sister for a nanosecond after she relayed the message. He had his phone out, his mind moving at lightening speed as his fingers dialed Mason. With a narrow glance at the sheriff's deputy who'd been redirected to handle the scene at the general store, he stepped outside and walked to his Jeep.

Mason answered in a lazy drawling voice that told Hawk more than words could that all was good in his friend's life. Too bad he was going to disturb that lovely interlude. But they had trouble.

When he started to explain, Mason got serious fast. While he relayed the message about the bombs, chemical warfare for clients, Mason made plans. When he mentioned the Empire State building, Mason was already moving. "We haven't been called in on this one, you know that."

"I do. But I can't leave. This is my sister, my hometown. From what I can see from the nonexistent law en-forcement, *no one* is going to be called in to handle this."

"You said the military were called?"

"No, I said the people on the streets were expecting them. So far there is nothing. I need confirmation the military are on their way, plus I need to go after Mia and her father."

"Of course you do." But Mason's voice was distant, already working the big picture. "How many of the squad are there or on the way?"

Hawk hesitated. "Swede for sure. I haven't called the rest."

"I think it's time you did. I'll call you back."

Hawk grinned. Now that was more like it. By the time he'd called his team and caught them up on the events, they were all in. God he loved them.

"From the look on your face, I'm assuming *something* is good news?" Eva said from beside him, hope in her voice.

"Not sure yet, but just talking to the guys, yeah, that's always good news."

"Are we going to Mia's place?"

"I am. You're going inside, tell the sheriff about your conver-sation with me."

She frowned. "I want to come with you."

He snagged her into a big hug and held her close. Then re-leased her. "Not happening and you know it. This is what I do."

"You don't have weapons or your team," she protested. "You can't go up against men with a truck load of weapons."

"Truckload?" he stared at his sister. "Maybe you should clue me in here a little more as to just what Gordon has going on?"

She shrugged. "I don't know much, but he had a new shipment brought in for the upcoming hunting season."

"Right." And mighty good timing. Then again, for a man who had a cache of weapons, hunting rifles weren't going to be of much interest. Unless he was desperate and they were readily available.

The deputy came back outside then. Hawk stood on the edge of the Jeep and asked him point blank when the army was arriving. The deputy shook his head. "Won't be any coming. The sheriff says he's handling it."

Hawk nodded, but inside...

What bullshit. He pulled his Jeep out of the lot and ripped down the main street. Handle it my ass. That sheriff wasn't going to handle anything. This wasn't something he could keep under wraps – at least not for long. Unless this was more misinformation.

Surely all this wouldn't be over something minor – would it?

No. Gerry's death said something so much bigger was going on.

CHAPTER 5

MIA CROUCHED BESIDE her father. He'd slipped into unconsciousness, his color wax, his body lying at an awkward angle. "Dad, can you hear me?"

"I only hit him over the head," he gunman said. "He dropped instantly but was conscious so he's not badly hurt."

"He hasn't been well. He was in a car accident a few months ago."

"It don't matter much," he paused, then added in a hard voice. "I'm either going to put a bullet in him, or he's going to get up and walk out of here. I can't be leaving witnesses."

She closed her eyes. Damn it. She squeezed her father's hand and caught back her gasp when he squeezed back. So very lightly but it was a definite attempt to let her know he was there.

"There is another solution," she said to the gunman.

"Yeah," he mocked. "And what's that?"

"I'll go with you, and my dad won't say anything to anyone because he'll know I'm with you."

"But he won't know cause he's out cold and he might just say something anyway," the gunman snapped. "Nice try though."

"Then as he doesn't know anything and he's injured and unconscious, leave him alone. He's already been through so much I doubt his body will handle much more." That truth hurt.

Where the hell was Hawk? If this asshole managed to escape with her as a captive, Hawk would never find her. And her father would die. He'd come close a few months ago. He was already weak. He might not survive this second trauma.

She glanced around the storehouse. Her father had promised he'd reduce stock and clean this place out. Instead it looked like he'd stockpiled *more*. He was a bit of an "end of the world junkie." Something else she'd tried to get him to see reason over, but he was who he was, and if he wanted to keep a ten year supply of canned food, who was she to argue?

She shifted her position so she was sitting on the ground. If the gunman stole all this food and supplies, he could hole up for years.

A sobering thought. She squeezed her father's hand again, trying to impart a sense of security, reassurance to him. But this time there was no answering response.

Her phone was still in her pocket. The gunman had either forgotten or didn't care. That last part scared the hell out of her.

"Why aren't you running away and hiding?" she asked cautiously. "That's what I'd do if my stash had been found."

"Why? They don't know it's me. Have no idea whose stash it is. Besides, I'm *not* leaving it all behind. And neither is it my only stash. The finished weapons are in a different location. And today is delivery day." The gun prodded her back. "I need that payout. No way in hell I'm losing that."

She closed her eyes. Shit. Shit. *Shit.*

"Ah, I see you fully understand the situation you're in now." He laughed. "A bullet for both of you would be much easier, wouldn't it? Well, I don't feel like making things easier on you. You and your pretty little world, you have no idea what's going on under the surface. You walk on people every day but think it's your right. Well, maybe it is. Just like I've been doing my thing in the caves below, thinking it's my right."

"It's not your right to hurt people. To make bombs to blow places up."

"What do you know with your fancy house and job and life-style? You've never fought for something worthwhile. Something major that is happening on a global scale." Now something fervent, almost fanatical filled his voice.

She watched him and wondered. "Is this a terrorist plot?"

"This is so much more than that." He laughed. "You wouldn't understand. You have everything, but have nothing important. No faith. No cause. No beliefs."

She mentally listed off the known terrorist groups. Not that the names mattered. They were so much the same. And all of them scared the crap out of her.

So did he.

"On your feet," he said in a hard voice. "It's time."

She hated to ask but forced the words out. "Time for what?"

She heard a heavy truck approach. Too heavy for the Jeep.

"Time to go."

He turned the gun on her father and she stepped in the way. "I'll go with you if you spare his life."

"You're coming anyway," he said in surprise. "So you have nothing to bargain with."

"I'll come willing. You won't have a fight out of me to worry about."

He studied her father's limp body then her then shrugged. "Whatever, but if you do, you get a bullet."

What was she doing? Please let Hawk get here fast.

HAWK WAS ON the main road when his phone rang. He pulled it out, clipped it to his dash and hit the speaker button. "I'm here," he growled. "What's new?"

"Maybe I should be asking you that," Swede said. "I'm about a half hour out. Do you have an update?"

"I do." In a terse voice he gave it to him. "I'm on the way to Gordon's place now. According to what Eva heard through Mia's phone, Gordon is injured and unconscious and Mia is trying to save him from a bullet. The gunman has Gordon's home cache as well now."

"Damn. Not good. That's a lot of weapons. What kind? Who are they for?"

"Mason is on it," Hawk said. "The thing is we're on the spot, and Mia is in trouble. I'm heading there now. I have to help."

"It's also going to be hours before anyone else is mobilized to this location."

Hawk snorted. "It's going to be hours before they get the intel they need in order to mobilize anything. What if this guy is so destructive right now because he has something going down? He said today is delivery day. He's not going to let anything get in his way."

"It already has," Swede said. "We need background on Gerry."

"Yeah, we do. I deliberately didn't even bring my laptop with me. And so far I haven't exactly had a half hour to search my phone for information."

"Na. Cooper is on it now. When you told me it was Gerry not Gordon I got him started. Gerry is a whole different issue. I don't like to think he came bringing trouble with him."

"He did." Hawk realized he hadn't filled him in on that part Gordon had shared. He quickly added in the rest of the information.

"Then we got bigger trouble than we first thought. We need the team and our gear."

"It's unofficial."

"Screw that. It's family."

Hawk pulled out into the passing lane and sped up to get past the panel truck ahead. It was trundling along at a slow pace like it had nothing to worry about. But it would be easy to hide weapons in it too. Now he was going to be looking at every vehicle like it was a terrorist bomb. Shit.

The turnoff was just up ahead, he went to brake then realized that the big truck behind him was slowing too. Damn it. He hit the gas and blew past the turnoff. The truck slowed more and turned onto Gordon's driveway. The house was in the back, set far under the grove of huge evergreen trees making for great camouflage. Also it was completely hidden from the road. He slowed, told Swede what was happening and pulled a U-turn on the road.

"I'm fifteen minutes away."

"Better make that five. She's not going to have much more than that."

He pulled the Jeep onto the driveway, going deep into the trees as far out of sight as he could. He shut off the engine and slipped out into the woods and started toward the house. There were no sounds. The house was silent. Everyone was in the back with the truck. He crept through the trees to the back of the house and realized there were indications of loading and unloading there. He eyed the front. He could sneak inside and see what was going on, but it would be harder to get out fast enough if things blew up.

And they were going to.

It was just how and what side the bodies would fall that concerned him.

Therefore…he crept to the far side of the house. One man stood on the side, a cigarette in his hand, a cell-phone to his ear, talking. "Yeah, we're going to load up in a few minutes. The remaining cache is about twenty minutes from here. An hour or so to load, then we should be on our way in just over two hours." He nodded. "Will do."

And he hung up. He turned to the others. "Let's lock and load. I said we'd be leaving town in two hours."

"And what about the girl and her father."

"Shoot them."

CHAPTER 6

M IA'S HEART STOPPED at his words. Since the arrival of the truck, the game had changed. There'd be no getting out of this mess now. She dove to the side of the shed but couldn't cover her father's body. Damn it. What could she do? Where was Hawk?

"I think we should take her with us. A hostage is always good. It stops the cops from storming us when they are worried about innocent lives." The snicker in his voice said a lot.

She took a deep breath and listened.

"Once they realize what we've got planned, they will throw their best at us anyway."

"Let them." The man with a snicker turned ugly. "Better yet, let's invite them over."

"Well, as they are likely to be there when we arrive."

"There's no law enforcement close by. None that count anywhere. Just the sheriff."

"Like he'd care. I think he could be bought off for a few hundred bucks?"

Mia listened to them argue. She had no idea who the authorities would send but given the location and type of problem she'd bet the military won. It's not like the neighboring towns had access to big city manpower.

Her vote was SEALs – as in Hawk. But not even he could handle this group on his own. Not with all the firepower these men had collected. She'd been arguing with her father since forever about his gun business. She didn't care if he did have a license. It still wasn't a smart business to have. But he was a big believer in the weapons being innocent and the people being guilty. He figured that a killer was going to kill no matter what the weapon. She turned back into the conversation.

"You're an idiot. With no law enforcement they'll bring in the military for that cache. So military it is. And not the SEALs, they are just a bunch of overrated assholes who think their shit don't stink like the rest of us."

"Why not the SEALs? Hell, we should rate enough for them," the speaker was irate at the slight.

"Not gonna happen." The other man's laugh turned ugly. "At least not until we start killing the American people. They'll notice us then. Besides, they're more water based, you know that."

She watched as the one skinny man shrugged, glanced her way, then added, "It would still be nice to have a warm body to snuggle up to tonight."

"Gross. I don't agree with rape, you know that."

As much as she loved hearing that, she struggled with the concept of a terrorist happy to blow up the American people in mass killings but didn't agree with rape.

"I can make her willing," the first man protested.

Mia felt her head flip flop from one to the other. Just the thought of what he'd do to make her willing…

"Like that's going to happen, Stan." The other man snorted. "No. She's just going to cause problems."

"Now, I have to shoot her, you said my name," Stan complained. "You know we weren't going to do that?"

"Do what? Talk to each other." The first gunman who'd forced her into the back turned to her and said, "He's Stan, the driver is George and I'm Dave." Then he turned back to the others. "Don't be stupid. We can't leave anyone alive. Whether they know our names or not. She's seen our faces, remember?"

With a disgusted look at the two men, he motioned to the stacks of boxes. "Load up. We have to grab the order and take it to the rendezvous." When they didn't move, he snapped, "Now."

The two men galvanized into action.

Mia sat huddled against the wall. She wished she could see them clearly enough to memorize their faces, like she'd committed their names to memory. They knew where she was, and it wasn't like she had a way to escape, but damn it, she wanted one. There was too much firepower here to fight off on her own. She glanced around. There were a few cracks in the shed where daylight snuck in, but they were between the metal strips. Her father had been lamenting the need to fix the storehouse for years, but it was backed against the cliff so even if she could get out, she couldn't get anywhere.

A small scratching sound came from directly behind, then something poked her. She twisted to see a hand come through the back wall. A large male hand. She grabbed it and squeezed. He squeezed back then tried to pull back but she couldn't let him. She didn't want to be alone. But he couldn't help her if she didn't let him go.

Biting her lip, she let go.

"Faster, we're wasting time, move it."

The men jumped to it, loading up crates and boxes faster.

Her heart pounded as she heard noises behind her. Could the men hear? But they were making so much noise themselves as they loaded up she could only hope they couldn't. And she had no idea how she could get out behind the damn shed if Hawk did get that hole open enough. She had no doubt that was who was here. It had to be Hawk. No one else would be foolish enough. Heart pounding, she silently urged him on. She kept twisting to see his progress behind her then to the men's progress in front of her. When she got a hard jab to her back, she spun and saw a corner of the metal sheeting lifted barley high enough for her head to go through. She wasn't going to get out there.

"Now," came the hoarse whisper.

Shaking her head but already trying to get through, she realized he was standing over top and lifting the edge of the sheeting up barely enough for her to wiggle under. Her shoulders were a tight squeeze, and with the rocks right there, she had no space to move. Who'd have thought her morning squirming through cave tunnels would hold her in good stead. She managed a little further then strong arms grabbed her under her arms and yanked her free. She scrambled to her feet and whispered, "My father."

DAMN. HAWK PEEKED under the sheet metal flap. He wasn't going to be able to save Gordon. But he had to try. They had seconds before the men would be coming for Mia. But Gordon was his friend. If there was anything he could do... Hawk quickly shoved Mia to the side and crawled in. Gordon's arm was only a couple of feet away, but he wasn't a small man. Hawk grabbed the arm and tugged the big man toward him. It was slow going, but he was gaining traction. Finally, he could grab under the back arm pit and he struggled backwards. Not being able to stand up, he couldn't get any leverage to pull.

Up ahead he could hear the men were laughing and joking. "Okay, that's the last box. Now the girl and get out of here."

"Wait, these damn boxes are going to shift. We can't have that. Come on. We have to spread them out. We'll need to repack when the bombs are loaded."

Hawk froze. Bombs?

He gathered his strength and dragged Gordon the last bit to the hole that was too damn small.

Mia jumped forward and pulled the metal sheeting back.

"I told you to run," he whispered.

"Not without you and my father."

He shook his head and dragged Gordon through the damn hole. "We're killing him, moving him like this."

"He has a chance this way. He has no chance against a bullet."

He couldn't argue that. Finally like a dam suddenly coming unstuck, Gordon slid through. Hawk grabbed his lax body and threw him over his shoulder. Mia bolted ahead of him toward the front.

"Psst," Hawk whispered and ran up the hill behind the shed. The men would be less likely to chase them if it was hard work. He checked to make sure Mia was following. She was now running behind him. He motioned for her to go ahead.

"We need to go up about five hundred yards then down to the road and come around. My Jeep is hidden in the trees."

Relief blasted across her face and she moved off in the direction he pointed.

CHAPTER 7

S HE COULDN'T HELP the panic firing her feet forward. The men were on their heels, they had to have noticed she'd escaped and it wasn't like their path was hidden. She knew they'd scuffed up the ground dragging her father out of there.

She peered through the trees. How far was five hundred yards? Had she passed that part? Surely he'd have said something. For the tenth time in half that many seconds she turned to glance at Hawk's progress. And marveled. He was running light on his feet, her father across his shoulders. He easily kept pace with her even as he studied the woods around them. He was looking for the best place to go down.

Good, she was ready to get off this ridge. She didn't like heights. She'd leave that part to him.

She moved forward as fast as she could and as quietly as she could. She'd bolted initially then figured she should stop sounding like an elephant on the rampage as she moved through the trees. If they followed, then they followed, but let it not be because she couldn't stay light enough on her feet.

"Turn up ahead at the fallen tree."

She didn't turn back. She stared at the largest deadfall tree she'd ever seen.

Turning toward it, she felt her feet shoot out from under

her. She managed to muffle her shriek but couldn't stay upright. She fell on her butt and did a fast downward slide.

At least she got to sit down. At the bottom she picked herself up and hid behind a tree. Then took a moment to clean off her clothes.

"Ready?" Hawk was already at her side, showing no signs of having fallen or needing a rest. He'd made it down that cliff without any visible stress. She, on the other hand, looked like she'd been pulled through the mud.

He waited until she straightened then said, with exaggerated calm, "If you're ready."

She admired his calm attitude and cool control. Whereas she was ready to scream and rampage at this point. She moved ahead of him and led the way. They shouldn't be far from the main road. If they could get onto that…they could get help.

But he said he had a Jeep. If that was available, they could get the hell away from here and contact the authorities. And her dad could get to the hospital. Not that he'd like her decision. He hated the damn places. She couldn't really blame him. God help the nurses when he woke up.

She came to a stop. Where was the Jeep? She spun round to glare at Hawk. But he pointed in the same direction as they'd been travelling. She kept up the brutal pace. Her body was saying it needed rest. And water. She'd used up one bottle of water spelunking and had left the rest in her truck. Too bad. She could really use some. This was hot work.

Looking back at him, still carrying her father, he walked on the forest floor, but he appeared to do so soundlessly. She understood the silence part but not the depth of his silence. It was fascinating. How could he walk on the dry underbrush and not make a sound?

"Take a left." His low deep voice startled her out of her rev-erie. Instinctively she followed his orders. She made her way around a bend, through a dip, then back up again.

"Left again."

Cutting a hard left, she came around a thick stand of brush and stopped. His black Jeep was parked in front of her. She started to shake with relief. Stupid really, they were a long way away from being safe.

She ran forward and tried to open the passenger door and realized of course it was locked. She raced back to Hawk, but he was already around the corner. He shifted her father's weight and dug the keys out of his pocket. He pushed the unlock button and she heard the locks disengage. She opened the door and hovered as he lowered her father to the back seat. He struggled with the straps for a long moment then had him buckled in. She saw what he'd done and raced to the other side to repeat it. Coming back around, she hopped into the front seat.

Hawk took his place behind the wheel and with a quick glance around, fired up the engine. Her panic rose as she heard the roar of the engine. They were going to be seen. Caught.

They had to hurry, but Hawk was moving slowly, carefully as he backed out of the hiding spot. Then he was down the driveway and turning onto the main road. He stopped.

"Go, go," she cried. "We're almost safe."

A big badass looking truck roared toward them. And came to a braking stop beside them. With windows rolled down, she realized it was a friend of Hawks. And good Lord what a friend. Huge, filling the cab and making the truck look just the perfect size for him. His face was hard. Lean. And damn cold.

A second man, smaller, leaner, sat in the shadows on the far side. She couldn't make out his features.

The conversation was curt and short. Then Hawk raced forward. She spun to see if his friend was following. But he turned into the driveway and hopped out.

"Didn't you warn them?"

Hawk looked at her in surprise. "About what?"

"The gunmen? The weapons' cache. That they hurt my father. Tried to kidnap me." She couldn't help herself. Her voice rose to a yell at the end.

"Oh that. They know."

Silence.

"So why are they getting out. We need to get help."

"Honey," he drawled, a smile on his face confusing her all the more. "They are the best damn help you'll ever get. They are part of my team."

She sat back. "They are SEALs?"

He nodded.

She swallowed. "But…"

"They know what they are heading into. I'll be going back as soon as I get your father to safety and you to the police."

Her mouth snapped shut. "I'm staying at the hospital. The sheriff can go there."

She felt his glance but stared mutely outside.

"You don't like the sheriff?"

"I don't know him," she said stiffly. "But it's not like they have anything to do with us."

"Maybe they haven't been around because there hasn't been any reason to be around."

"True."

"What aren't you telling me?"

"Nothing specific. I just don't like him."

He nodded and stayed quiet. Good. She really didn't want to explain the entire town's vantage point of the local law enforcement. He was right in that there was no need to have the law any closer and in fact, she was damn glad there wasn't as then she'd have to see them more often. She had no idea where the grudge came from. Well, maybe she did at that. Her father. Because he sold guns. That was likely to have set him against the authorities a long time ago, and that road had just never straightened up. He really didn't like the current sheriff. Called him a pompous ass. So yeah, she likely had been influenced by her father.

She twisted in her seat and glanced back to check on him. His breathing was shallow. Hoarse. He didn't look very good. Stretching out a hand, she reached out and stroked his arm. His skin was cool. She bit her lip, tears coming to her eyes. He'd been through so damn much lately. It was hard not to wonder if he'd hit the final hurdle.

The hospital was a good half hour away. They could have called the ambulance, but she knew it was often slower than driving straight through on their own.

"Swede has called the hospital. They are expected us." He pulled into the turning lane at the traffic light.

"Swede?"

"The one driving the truck back there."

"Oh. Is he Swedish?"

"No. He's actually Norwegian."

"That makes no sense."

He laughed. "His nickname comes from a completely different source than his heritage."

She wanted to ask what that was but the hospital was just ahead. He pulled up outside the emergency doors. They opened and two men with a gurney raced out. Before she'd had a chance to explain, her father was loaded up and wheeled inside.

"You must have pull to make them jump like that," she muttered.

"It's all about knowing what to say," he said comfortably. "Go deal with the paperwork. I'm heading back."

"Back?"

He nodded, his face set in grim lines. "Back to your father's house. We need to capture those bastards before they can do any more damage."

And just like that he was gone.

THERE WAS NO sign of Swede's truck when he pulled into Gordon's driveway. Then Hawk didn't really expect there to be any. His friend was too damn smart for that. Not to mention he loved that truck. There was no way he'd put it in harms way if he could avoid it.

Now Shadow, his passenger, well he couldn't be seen at the best of times. Hawk parked the Jeep where he'd parked it before and got out. Within seconds there was a loud Hawk's call overhead. He responded with a low key one of his own. The men converged on him.

"No sign of the truck. We've called it in."

"It was missing a plate when I saw it," Hawk mentioned.

"If they are smart they will have put one on by now. The license plate off Gordon's truck is missing. The authorities are watching for it."

"Anything left behind?"

Swede shook his head. "Nothing in the house. Nothing in the shed. Any idea where the bombs were cached?"

"No. In a cave. Somewhere. And this place is riddled with them. The area is popular with spelunkers from all over the world."

"Then they could be anywhere," Shadow said in a low voice. "This area is mapped. We'll need to grab a copy and look for the most likely option."

Hawk's cell phone vibrated in his pocket. Mia. He answered the call. "How's your father?"

"Alive, thanks to you," she answered quietly. "Thank you. Are your friends okay?"

Hawk's gaze slipped across Swede and Shadow's faces. "Both of them are standing in front of me. The truck was gone when they arrived, so the gunmen snuck out while we were going cross country."

"Damn."

"We'll find them. The authorities have been notified."

"I know. Look. It's probably nothing, but I was caving this morning and thought I saw something. At the time it didn't occur to me it was important, and I was with a group of six of us so didn't think about it much until I heard the gunmen talking about the missing cache."

"That makes sense but what does that have to do with the cave and whatever you saw?"

"I saw a bullet casing," she said. "I even picked it up. Just never said anything because we were leaving right away."

"What kind of bullet?" he asked, his voice hard.

"I'm not sure," she said apologetically. "I think it was from a rifle."

"That's a military gun." Hawk's gaze locked on Swede. Both his friends had frozen as he listened to Mia's voice. "Do they know you found it?"

"I don't think so. Unless they were watching me." Her voice rose. "They couldn't have been in the cave watching me, could they?"

"I doubt it. Chances are they'd have shot you if they had."

"But there were six of us," she reminded him. "If one person went missing that was one thing. Six is quite a different story."

He pondered that. "Did they ask you about guns while you were captive?"

"Not really. He did search me, but not very thoroughly. I had the bullet in my jeans pocket with my cellphone and he didn't take that either."

"That's odd." It's one of the first things he'd have removed.

"That's how Eva heard the conversation. Remember."

"Yeah, I do. We're going to see if we can find that bomb cache the men were talking about. Especially if today is delivery day."

"Let me come."

"No," he said instantly. "There's no way. You stay with your father."

"I know the cave system. If there is anything to find, I can help you find it. I was training for search and rescue missions for the spelunkers here. The place is a maze."

"Still not happening," he said. "You were in trouble, now you're safe."

"But you're not going to be if you go in alone."

Humor tinged his voice as he replied, "I'm pretty sure we

can find our way."

Frustrated silence filled the line. "And if I have to come and rescue you?"

He laughed. "That's not going to happen."

"But I can show you where I found the bullet. That will save time so you'll know where to start."

He frowned. "You can tell me where you found it."

"Hardly."

"You could."

"Okay." And she proceeded to rattle off the sting of caves she'd gone through and where she'd found the bullet. At least approximately. "There, does that help?"

He frowned thinking about it. "You could mark it on the map."

"I could, but then you'd have to come here and then go back down there."

"I'm sure you can scan it in and email it," he said.

"Damn it, why won't you let me go?"

"It's too dangerous." Hawk held the phone away from his ear as she let out a yell of frustration.

"If it's dangerous for me, how is it not dangerous for you?"

"It might be dangerous for us, but we're used to it."

Silence. "Do you really think doing search and rescue work is *not* dangerous?"

"You're not up against guns on a regular basis and we are."

"I've handled guns since I was old enough to carry one."

"But you still got yourself captured," he reminded her. "We can't afford to look after you."

That earned him a cursing. He grinned, she was too much fun to piss off but he had to go. "Send me a map of the cave system and give us an idea where to start."

And he clicked the phone off.

"Who is that?" Shadow asked.

"Mia. She's Eva's best friend and Gordon's daughter."

"Little Mia," Swede asked in astonishment. "Did I hear she's doing search and rescue work?"

Hawk nodded. "And she's not so little now."

"What was that about a bullet?"

He explained to the men. "We need a map of the system then we can get going and take a look." Swede looked up at the sky. "And the sooner the better. The weather is turning. We need to gear up if we're going un-derground."

"From where?"

Hawk opened his phone. "Mia, we need gear."

"And?"

"Does your father have any in his house? I don't want to just help myself without asking you," he said awkwardly.

"You saved his life, I don't think he'd mind if you borrowed stuff from the house or the shop to go save the world," she said and hung up.

He couldn't place the sounds he'd heard in the background while she'd been talking on the phone. He filled the others in and started toward the shed. "Let's check in here first."

"We already have. There's not much but overstock from the store."

"Any guns or ammo left?"

They shook their heads. "Not sure what all was here to begin with, but it's been pretty well emptied out."

Hawk took a quick glance around. Nodded and turned to the house. "We can go through the store if we need more."

"Let's hope he has the headlamps. A trip into town to buy equipment is going to slow us down."

Going through Gordon's house yielded very little. A few water bottles but that was all.

"He wasn't into caves apparently."

"He was a hunting nut."

Shadow nodded. "We need to check the store."

A screeching sound of brakes slamming hard had them all running for cover.

An old dilapidated truck pulled into the driveway and drove up to the house. Mia hopped out. "Thanks Cory." She motioned to her truck. "I'll be fine now."

The driver waved and with a squeal as his gears shifted, backed down the driveway.

She turned to face them. And kicked her chin up a notch.

CHAPTER 8

"I 'VE CALLED THE Bangor brothers. They are dropping off a couple of sets of harnesses," she rushed to say before Hawk could interrupt and yell at her. Her gaze went from one man to the other. "If we leave now we'll have a few hours of daylight. In the caves, time won't matter as it's all darkness anyway. We won't be hampered by a lack of daylight."

She stepped forward and held out her hand. "You must be Swede."

Swede shook her hand and nodded.

With her hand still outstretched, she walked to Shadow. "I'm Mia. Thank you for helping."

Shadow, quiet as ever, stepped forward and with a soft drawl said, "My pleasure. I'm sorry about your father. He's a good man."

And that was when she realized these men had met her father. Not just Hawk but the others as well. "He is a good man," she whispered. "He didn't deserve this."

"And your uncle?" Shadow asked. "What can you tell us about him?"

She shrugged. "Not much. He and my father were estranged for over thirty years. Then all of a sudden he shows up wanting to make peace. Dad never thought anything of it. He opened his door and let him back into his house and his life."

Shadow nodded. "What did your uncle do for a living?"

"Apparently he was down on his luck when he showed up at Dad's house. Part of the reason he let him in, I think. Dad has always been a softie."

"And then he started working at the store?" Shadow asked.

She nodded. "It gave me more time as I'd been helping out a lot more since Dad's accident."

His voice quiet, Hawk said, "How did the accident happen?"

"He was driving on the highway and some idiot ran him off the road."

The three men exchanged glances. She frowned. "What are you thinking?"

"That it was all a little too convenient," Swede suggested.

"In what way?"

"He gets run off the road, your father is injured, a long lost brother shows up needing work and before you know it there's a cache of weapons found and all hell breaks loose."

The thoughts ran through her mind. "Do you think Gerry was helping with bombs?"

"Was he the type?" Hawk asked curiously. "You haven't said anything as to what he was like. Or not like. How did you feel when he showed up?"

"I was happy for Dad's sake. But…" She stopped, hating to say anything against the dead man.

"But what?" prompted Swede.

"But… I didn't like him. I didn't like the avariciousness I heard from his everyday words or his constant assessing looks at my father, the shop, the house. As if to say if something happened to Dad, he'd be happy to step into his shoes. But he'd never fill them." She ran a hand through her hair. "He wasn't half the man Dad is."

The others nodded. "Then for the moment we'll assume he had something to do with this as the one terrorist implied. That his death was a falling out among thieves."

"What a thought."

"Have you any better hypothesis?"

Shadow's soft voice belied something else entirely. A sidelong glance his way confirmed her initial impression. That man handled danger like a baker handled bread dough.

And Swede. The big man looked like he'd used full size trees as toothpicks and snap them in half when he was done. But Hawk, there was something so implacable in his visage, she wondered if he wasn't the most dan-gerous. "No," she said in a quiet voice. "I don't have a clue what's going on."

A car drove in as she finished speaking. "That's Paul." She walked over and talked to her friend. He got out and unloaded the gear from the trunk. "Thanks for this, Paul."

He nodded. "Not an issue. Bring it back when you're done." She smiled her thanks as he pulled away.

Once he was out of sight, she turned to the others. "Ready?"

A scant half hour later, she was directing them to the turn off she'd taken first thing in the morning. The shadows from the tall trees cast the entrance in darkness. Only she'd been here many times over. She turned on her headlamp and led the way in. They were fully geared for anything, and like this morning, she hoped for nothing but a nice hike. If they were so lucky.

As they walked, she studied the men and realized they moved easily, fit and with lethal smoothness. Like Hawk, they made no noise as they walked.

In contrast, she felt like an elephant with every step she took. No matter how much she tried, the leaves still crackled under her feet.

"You're trying too hard. Instead of walking on the ground," Hawk said, correctly interpreting her frustration, "step inside the ground and be one with it."

She stopped and considered what he was saying then closed her eyes and stepped again. Her steps were softer. More in tune. Good. Well, better at least.

They entered the first cave, and she took the lead across the same cavernous space she'd walked this morning. And led them to the other cave and on and on. By the time they were at the tunnel, and she had to squirm through on her belly, she was comfortable with her companions' skill. They took to this like they likely took to every other challenge. Although Swede might find this part of the journey a little small. "This next section is tight," she warned. "So suck in your guts."

And she dove into the tight channel. By the time she made it through, dirt falling down on her face and neck and coughing out as much dust as she could, she struggled to her feet in the last cavern – the one where she'd found the bullet – and reached for her water bottle. She was still drinking when the others crawled out behind her.

Swede was covered. In fact, as she watched him come out, she realized he must have ploughed the tunnel wider with those damn shoulders of his. Shadow came behind him and made the journey look easy. And it probably was.

"So Swede, did you make it big enough I can walk through on the way back?"

The big man, now dusty with sand, spat and gave a chuckle.

"You should have let me lead. I'd have made it easier for you this time too."

She laughed and motioned to the far side. "It's in this cave that I found the bullet."

"Where?" Hawk was all business. Since standing up, his gaze had been steadily clocking the distance, the walls, the type of dirt on the walls, the height of the ceiling, etc. Such awareness she hadn't seen before.

Amazing.

She gave herself a good shake and walked to where she'd seen the small object. It was on the far side. She bent and pointed where it had lain.

Hawk studied the ground, then kicked the area with his boot. There was a small metallic sound. He bent down and ran his fingers through the loose dirt. And pulled up two more casings. He straightened, rolled them through his fingers. And nodded. "Likely the same gun that killed Gerry."

"I'm surprised they shot him at the store," she said. "Why not down here?"

"Why down here?"

She shrugged. "I don't know. So no one would find him."

"How many times have you been here in the last few days?"

She frowned. "Twice."

"And other people you know, how many were likely here?"

She winced. "Point taken. There's possibly been a dozen or more."

"So hardly out of the way. If they knew this area was mapped, they knew they'd likely be found and way earlier than they'd want to be."

"I suppose."

"Besides, this way it points to your father being guilty."

She gasped. "I never thought of that." She glanced around. "So why the casings here? Target practice?"

"Anything is possible." Swede looked at the far wall and pointed. "Look."

Sure enough on the far side were a series of circles chalked on the cave wall.

"Over here."

The others turned to where Shadow stood about twenty feet away. He pointed to the ground.

Walking over to stand beside the others, she glanced at the ground and realized she was staring at another set of casings. "Rifle?"

"Automatic."

"Now that we know we're in the right place, spread out and see what else you can find."

"This isn't where the cache was found," she protested.

"No, it might not be but the men were here."

"Then they didn't come the same way we did." She was positive about that.

The men stopped and looked at her. "Why?"

"Because you're not going to haul any of the weapons or bomb making equipment all through here. And there's no easy access for hauling it out."

Hawk's eyebrows shot up. "Right. Suggestions."

"Yes. I think the next cavern over has a double entrance with a slightly different access point. There was a lot of talk about it on my last trip. There used to be a long hike to get to it, but from what I understand, there are now truck tracks to the entrance."

"Can we get there from here?"

"And if so, why didn't we go that way this time?"

"Because I don't know how to find it from the outside," she said in exasperation. "This place is riddled with different tunnels."

"But you know how to get from here to there?" Swede asked her in surprise. "How does that work?"

"I don't know for sure, I know the general route, but that looks likely." She moved around Shadow and pointed to the floor in front of a small tunnel. "It's also seen recent traffic. I don't remember seeing these tracks earlier today."

"So you think someone came through from the other side today?"

"It's possible. It's also possible I missed it. I was thinking more of getting home than checking out footsteps." She crouched in front of the tunnel. "It's partly hidden, and we stopped before entering this one this morning as time was running out."

"So if you'd had enough time, would you have gone further?" Swede asked.

"Oh definitely." She stood up.

"It's a popular through fare? Do you file your trips?"

She nodded. "I go with several of the local club. We always file a trip plan."

He nodded. "Good. Let's go." He nodded to the tunnel. "Do you want to lead?"

She grinned. "Absolutely." Then stepped back. "But Swede makes it much easier if I go behind him."

Shadow laughed. "She's got your number."

With a roll of his eyes, the big man dropped to his knees and crawled inside the tunnel. It was big enough for him to squeeze through with difficulty. She fell into step behind him.

This tunnel was longer than the others she'd been in.

When Swede stopped, she halted in place. But they were still inside the tunnel. She waited but he didn't move. She reached over and grabbed his foot and gave it a shake. He reached a hand back in warning.

And she understood. Someone was up in front. Someone like the gunmen. She settled down to wait.

And wait. The temperature in the tunnel was surprisingly hot. It had been cool at the start, but full as it was now with large male bodies generating a tremendous amount of heat, it was getting overheated.

Her body ached from being on her knees hunched over. She shifted slightly and then froze. Sounds carried like a shot through the tunnel.

She could hear voices. Were they approaching? Shit. The other men hadn't made a move. Only her. What an idiot she was.

She took several deep open mouthed breaths. Trying to still the sense of panic.

The thought of being caught in here forever...well that was enough to make anyone panic. Why the men couldn't go forward and catch these bastards, she didn't know. Just when she'd given up trying to stay quiet and needing to move, Swede scrambled ahead and was suddenly gone.

Hawk was behind her. He gave her a hard shove and she scrambled to get out of the way. At the entrance she slipped to the left while her eyes adjusted to the different light.

The other two men bolted through the entrance and raced

after Swede. She didn't even understand where he'd gone, but he wasn't in front of her. Her gaze searched the gloom. Was he?

And if he wasn't, where was he? And the others? Had they raced into unknown territory like that? Were they nuts? They might be SEALs but they weren't completely infallible. Surely.

She used the wall to stand up while she tried to adjust her gaze to the off lighting. And gasped. The whole room was empty. She ran to the far side where the next tunnel opened. There was no one as far as she could see there either. But it was the only route out so they'd had to have gone down there. Shit. She wanted to click her headlight on so she could see but didn't want to bring any unwanted attention her way.

The safest thing she could do was keep herself snugged up against the wall where she was out of sight and out of the way.

Except…how long was she supposed to stand here in the dark.

"Well, well well, what do we have here?"

She spun around and a hand clapped over her head, a cloth came over her mouth. She struggled, but her head swam and clouds filled her mind. Her body crumpled but never hit the ground.

"MIA?"

Hawk circled the large room. He'd left her in the tunnel. Where the hell was she now? Swede and Shadow were following the trail of goods to the exit. He'd doubled back for her. Where the hell was she?

"Mia?" he called out louder. But there was no answer. He made it back to the opening of the tunnel and froze. He lifted his nose and sniffed the air harder. Chloroform.

Shit.

He turned his light on bright and glanced at the ground. Footsteps where she'd been standing, her weight strong, her back leaned against the wall, her heels dug into the dirt. Then scuff marks as she struggled.

Her heels dragged along the tunnel as she was pulled back-wards. For how long? He raced behind the tracks. She couldn't have been taken far. There hadn't been time. Less than ten minutes.

He ran easily, tracking the trail.

And came to the large cavern. He slid out into the cavern and against the closest wall. Nothing rustled in the darkness. Nothing moved. And there were no shadows that hadn't been there earlier. No sign of her.

He raced to the small tunnel. It would be much harder to take her all the way back. But there was the evidence that just that was in progress. She was being dragged. Likely her arms over her head and dragged. A hard way to go. They'd have to be strong. Then again, Mia was slim. Long and lean but light.

Anyone used to making such physical effort wouldn't have had a problem carrying her.

He dove into the tunnel and scrambled through to the other side. Still no sign of her. In the background was an odd scraping sound. He moved faster. The closer he got, the louder the sound of someone being dragged became. He'd found her. He had to save her before she was dragged all he way out. If they got her into a vehicle, it would be that much harder to rescue her.

And that wasn't going to happen.

She was too sweet. Too attractive. And damn if he wasn't

interested.

As in damn interested.

But he had to save her first.

The drag noises stopped.

He froze. Voices up ahead. Shit.

CHAPTER 9

H ER HEAD ACHED, and her blood pounded so loudly she could hear nothing but the pulse that flooded her veins. She groaned. Then heard voices in the dimness of her mind.

"Why the hell is she awake?" growled one male. "I gave her enough to knock out a damn horse."

"Whaaat?"

"Shut the fuck up."

A strange sound whispered through her consciousness. What was that? It was a low level hum dragging across her skin. The sound aching deep inside as it grated inside her ears. It was like a rubbing sound. And it wouldn't stop.

What the heck was it? She tried to roll over. But couldn't. She tried again. And the drag sounds were worse. Her head responded with a heavy ache. Why couldn't she figure out the noise in her head? And what was it going to take to make it stop. She moved her arms. And cried out.

"Shit."

Someone was talking to her? "Who's there?" she turned to ask, yet only a broken whimper made it past her lips.

And of course there was no answer.

She tried to move her arms again. Pain ripped through her – again. Groaning, she rolled over and immediately dust filled her mouth starting her coughing. She spat and struggled to sit up. Her arms were yanked hard.

She cried out as her body was pulled backward.

And she realized she was being dragged. She was hearing her body scraping along the ground.

She tried to pull back.

"Like hell you're getting away." He jerked hard and she went flying forward. "Stop struggling, you're not going anywhere."

"And she's not going with you," a strange voice snapped.

A male jumped over her and suddenly her arms were free. She groaned as they fell to her side. The pain was excruciating. She struggled to pull them free of the ropes. Groggy, she stood up and watched Hawk in an all out fight against a stranger in front of her. With a hand on the wall, she managed to stand up. She was so damn shaky it was hard to stay on her feet once she was vertical.

She gasped, trying to regain her senses. And suddenly Hawk was at her side. She tried to see behind him, but he blocked her view. "Don't move. I don't know what happened, but I think you were given something to knock you out."

Outraged, she tried to take a step but listed to the side. He snagged a hold of her and held her close. "Take it easy."

"I'm trying to. Did you kill him?" She peered over her shoulder but couldn't see the man.

"No, I just knocked him out." His breath was warm against her forehead.

"I don't think you did a very good job then, he's gone."

Hawk spun around. And she had a clear view confirming the man's escape.

"Shit." Hawk glared into the darkness where the man disappeared.

She tried to push him away. "Go after him. I'll be fine."

His snort was anything but pleasant. "I left you alone last time and look what good that did."

"It wasn't your fault. I was hiding in the dark. I should have been safe."

"But you weren't. We were following the group ahead of us but missed someone hiding in the shadows. Shadow will be pissed when he realizes that."

"Why?"

"He prides himself on those."

"Shadows or men hiding in the shadows?"

"Both."

She tried to step back and stand on her own two feet but couldn't quite make it. She slumped against him again, loving the strength that held her so easily. He was a man's man. And of course that made him a ladies' man.

"You're not quite ready to throw this off just yet."

A weird echoing birdcall whistled through the cavern.

"Good, that's Swede," he said.

"Sending a bird call, isn't that a little melodramatic."

"Efficient. We send different messages back and forth using the calls. Each one means something different."

"Cool." She straightened up and managed to look around. "Does that mean your friends are coming back now?"

"Yes."

Sure enough the men burst through the cavern.

"Mia, are you all right?" Swede asked, striding over to her.

She nodded. "I am now, thanks to Hawk."

Hawk explained.

"Do you think he's on the run or waiting for us up ahead?" Mia asked in a low voice as the men scattered, leaving the two of them behind with Swede.

"He's running. They are late for a rendezvous. We lost them on the other tunnel but heard where they are going. And apparently it's not a US monument that they are after but a bridge instead. The Golden Gate Bridge."

A moment of silence filled the air as they each contemplated the concept of the bridge being bombed.

"Jesus," she whispered quietly, sagging heavier against Hawk. "We have to go after them."

"Shadow is on it. We are going back to the vehicle and will follow."

She shook her head. "We're going to lose them. Let's go." And she tried to walk forward but sagged to her knees.

Swede gave a muffled exclamation and snatched her up into his arms. "Shadow is going to try and hitch a ride up ahead."

Hawk led the way back to the vehicle.

"You should have left me behind," Mia said. "You could have caught him."

They reached the entrance to the cave in time to hear a vehicle driving closer.

"Damn it, he's getting away," Mia cried.

Only the vehicle was approaching them, not driving away.

"Or his partners are coming to pick him up."

Hawk melted into the bushes. Swede stepped in the shrubbery, keeping her out of harm's way and watched. She struggled to stand up, but Swede wouldn't let her. Realizing arguing was fruitless, she relaxed back.

Shots crackled through the air. The car engine revved then

changed as if the vehicle was backing up. And gunned it. It disappeared in the distance, the sounds quickly fading.

Swede stepped back onto the road and strode quickly forward. They turned around the bend up ahead and she gasped.

Hawk was squatting beside the body lying on the road.

He straightened as they approached. "It's the man who attacked Mia."

Swede lowered her to the ground and with Hawk's help, she walked closer and stood over the man. Now that she was in the natural sunlight, she could see his features. "He was at Dad's."

"Yes, he was."

"He's the one who wanted to keep me. The other guy called him Stan."

Both men stared at her. She frowned at them. "I told you, didn't I? Or maybe you heard it." She shook her head trying to clear her thoughts. "The one wanted to take me with him to keep him warm at night, but the other man said he had no tolerance for rape. And this guy," she motioned to the dead man, "said he'd *make* me willing."

The matching frowns deepened.

"You didn't share that part."

"Oh." She shrugged. "It doesn't matter now."

"But it does as it explains why you didn't get a bullet when he saw you."

She brightened. "Right."

"Let's go," Hawk said, motioning in the direction of the vehicles. "You need to be checked over and we need to move it."

"You're going after the men?"

They just turned those flat gazes her way. Of course they were going after them.

HAWK WALKED TO Gordon's bed. And found the old man awake. Good.

"Damn it's good to see you. And good timing," Gordon managed to get out. "I owe you my life."

"You owe me nothing but I could sure use details. What the hell's going on?"

Shifting uneasily, Gordon said, "I don't know the whole story but have an idea." He raised a shamed gaze to Hawk. "My brother is involved."

"Was involved." Hard cold clipped, Hawk wasn't going to allow for any misconceptions here. "He was shot with a single bullet to the head."

Gordon nodded. "I know. And...I'm sorry, but now that I know what I know, I'm not surprised."

"Tell me." Hawk stood and waited. What he heard was a bigger development on the bit Mia had shared. "So Gerry came back expressly to set this scenario up? To collect the stash and when the cops found it, he told his cohorts about your stockpile?"

"I think so. The men who kicked the shit out of me had a good laugh at me being set up. Then again they had a good laugh at killing my brother too."

"Any idea what their plans are?" Gordon asked.

"Golden Gate Bridge. Water attack of some kind." Gordon leaned back against the headboard and closed his eyes. "Is Mia okay?"

"Yeah, she's here in the hospital but she's going to be fine."

"The army was in to see me," Gordon said. "I told them everything."

"And the sheriff, did he show up?"

The snort said it all. "I haven't seen him but apparently he was here. Didn't bother talking to me though."

"Maybe you weren't awake yet?"

"I was awake. I heard the fuss in the hallway. He was doing the minimum he had to before walking away. More than happy to dump this in someone else's hands. Might be the Feds taking it over too as these guys came from three states for this and will be heading to California for the attack."

"Makes sense," said Hawk in neutral tones. "Who found the cache?"

"Local man – ex-military," Gordon said. "When his boys found it, him being who he is and all...he called in his buddies and that was that. Now it will likely be a joint operation."

"Minus the sheriff."

They both smiled at that. Hawk checked his watch. He was late. He'd hoped to see Mia but he was out of time.

CHAPTER 10

"I'M FINE. I just want to go home," Mia told the doctor earnestly. "I promise I'll rest."

"And how are you going to get there?" he said, writing something on the tablet. "You shouldn't drive."

Mia frowned, wishing her head would clear. "I don't have my own wheels here anyway."

"If you take a cab or get picked up, then fine."

She brightened. "Thank you."

The doctor walked out of the room, leaving her to put her jacket and shoes back on. She'd have some paperwork to do before she was finally released, but she was looking forward to getting home. But first, she had to see her father.

She walked into her father's room as Hawk rushed out. She brightened. He hadn't left without saying good-bye. Her instinctive thought. After all, she had nothing to offer him. Especially him. And especially being her. She wasn't close to being a bombshell, and she'd heard about the SEAL life. From many sources. Enough to know it was the truth.

She'd had boyfriends, but she hadn't had a long string of them. She preferred quality over quantity. And understood Hawk could have both in as many forms as possible.

She could never compete.

And he was…well, he was just so much.

She was such an idiot. Now if only she could get through this gracefully.

She sighed and gave him a small wave good-bye. "Thanks again for the rescue," she said in a shamefaced voice as he came to a stop beside her. "Normally I'm the one doing the rescuing."

"Sometimes even the toughest of us need a little help." He patted her on the shoulder. "You stay here and heal. I've got to run." He walked away backwards with a final caution, "Please stay out of trouble."

And he was gone.

Damn it.

"Are you going to come back?" she called out. Then winced. Talk about subtle. Not. Where was that wish for a graceful good-bye, head high, classy finish? Snort.

He turned enough to see her but didn't stop moving. "Not for awhile."

Her face fell. Her heart sagged and her body just plain hurt.

She turned away and saw her father awake. Bursting into tears, she raced to give him a big hug.

"I'm so glad you're okay," she said through her sobs.

"I'm so very glad you and Hawk were both there to help."

"You mean Hawk. He rescued both of us," she admitted.

"Good. Glad he did." Her father reached up and rubbed his temple. "My head is pounding. It's going to be days before I feel up to opening the store."

"Are you still going to?" she asked quietly.

He raised an eyebrow. "Why wouldn't I?"

"Well, your brother was shot in the store, it was ransacked, the guns were stolen and your cache at home was also stolen."

He shrugged. "It was all insured."

She nodded but inside it bothered her. "I'm not sure I like the idea of you selling guns anymore."

"You never did." He pursed his lips and studied her. "Nervous now? That's not like you."

"Watching those men..." She shuddered. "It did make me think."

He shook his head. "It's not the guns. It's the people–"

"People who use them." She groaned. "Yeah, I know."

"Lucky you, you're free to leave," he said. "What are you going to do now?"

"As you're fine and safe here, I'm going home. I got a pass from the doctor as long as I rest." She stood up and reached over to hug him. "Love you, Dad."

"Love you too, Mia." He smiled up at her. "This will be a bad memory soon."

"I hope so."

With a small wave, she turned and walked out. Her energy was flagging. She needed to grab a cab. Outside she realized it was late. How was it she hadn't understood that? Just staring out at the dark night she realized she probably should have stayed for the night. But that was fear talking.

Better to go home and face it. Now, should she go to her place or to her father's house? No, she wasn't going back there for a while. She needed time so she wouldn't see her father's body lying crumpled on the ground every time she was there.

Outside the hospital, she stood at the front doors and stared across the parking lot. There were cabs waiting on the front curb. She walked over to one, but it drove away as she approached.

A truck drove between her and the next taxi. She tried to

walk around it but a man hopped out. She shifted out of his way.

The man called out to her. "Excuse me."

She spun and looked at him, "Yes."

"I think this is for you." He held out a package.

She frowned. "From who?"

"A guy in a black Jeep."

Her face lit up. Hawk. "Oh," she said hopefully and reached out to take it. "Thank you so much for delivering–"

She never saw the blow, never felt the air cut off from her lungs. Nor did the pain hit her awareness quickly. Instead it was like a slow motion movie as she watched her body fall into his waiting arms. She knew something was wrong but couldn't seem to connect the weird grip on her neck with the numbness of her legs.

His voice, concerned and helpful, called to her. "Oh dear. Are you all right? Here, let me help you up."

She was boosted into the back seat of the truck where she toppled forward into the foot well. Her head hit the seat cushion and bounced off to slide to the floor. She lay there, her eyes open, her brain aware, her mind no longer functioning.

The truck engine turned over.

"Is she okay?"

"Yeah, for now. We'll have to find out who she's talked to and take care of them as well. But for the moment, the issue is contained."

"Can't leave any loose ends."

"A couple of days are all we need. Less if things go as planned."

"Should just dump her in the river. Be done with it."

"Have to figure out what she knows first. Who she's told.

Can't leave that to chance. After that, we'll shut her up permanently."

"Should have done it before she could talk. Damn Stan."

"Yeah, he's always been one for taking a little bit of a bonus for himself. But we needed the extra manpower, and he was someone we'd used before."

"Now we'll need a couple of new men when we hit the docks."

"There's lots of casual labor around there. People who don't ask too many question."

"Good."

Mia lay in the back, the words rolling through her brain. She wanted to retain them but they flitted in and out. Making sense then not making any sense. Between the rest of the events of the day her brain wanted to shut down.

"Settle in, we've got a decent ride ahead of us," the stranger called back to her. "You won't be leaving this truck until we hit our destination."

Her eyes drifted closed. *Please not.*

All she'd wanted to do was go home and rest. Instead she was in trouble. And she had no way of calling for help.

HAWK WOKE FROM his power nap after ten minutes. Perfect. With Shadow driving, they were still making good time and he was revving up ready to go.

"Glad to hear Gordon's doing well," Shadow said as he drove Hawk's Jeep down the highway behind Swede's truck. "He took a pretty good knock to his head."

"I am too." Hawk pulled out his phone and checked his messages. "Shit. There are several missed calls from him." He quickly called Gordon. "Hey, sorry I missed your calls. Is everything okay?"

"No. There's no sign of Mia. She left just after you to go home as the doctor gave her the okay, but she's not answering her phone and I've had a friend check both my house and hers and there's no sign of her. I'm calling her phone constantly but there's no response."

"What? Why did she leave?" He ran his fingers through his hair in frustration. "Maybe she went to my sister's place."

"No, Eva's looking for her. The last anyone can place her is here in front of the hospital. A cabbie thought she was coming toward him for a ride but a truck stopped and a guy got out. He said she appeared to be smiling and talking to him so he ignored her. When he looked up again, the truck and Mia were gone."

Gordon's voice dropped. "Damn it Hawk. What's the chance those guys decided they couldn't afford any loose strings?"

"But there are loose strings. You're alive. I'm alive. She's only one of many. Maybe he's a friend of hers." Hawk's heart raced as his mind reached for more reasonable explanations and came up empty. "Shit."

"I know. Where are you?"

"On the hunt."

"Make sure you're looking for my little girl at the same time. She's quite likely to be the catch at the end of the day."

Hawk glared at his phone. He'd turned the volume down low when they'd been trying to get away from the killer, and he'd forgotten to turn it back up again. He couldn't believe he missed the calls.

Would it have helped to have known earlier? Maybe not, but at the same time he couldn't not consider it. He'd been there at the hospital with her. Why hadn't she said she was heading home? He'd told her to stay and heal. She could have said something then. Then again he'd also told her to stay out of trouble. Why the hell hadn't he taken the time to drive her home?

Because he was after the terrorists and she was supposed to be safe. But he should have made *sure* she was safe. Not assumed she was because she was in the hospital.

And he was too damn attracted to her. It threw off his thinking. She was something. But *he* wasn't what Gordon would want for his little girl. Truly, Hawk couldn't blame him for thinking that.

Hawk had hardly led the type of life anyone would want for their daughter. So he had to stay away. She didn't appear to be interested in him more than her best friend's brother, but then again he hadn't given her any opening. She was strong and enduring and he loved that. It was qualities he'd seen in his team but never looked for in a woman. Then his relationships were the opposite of that. On purpose. He wasn't ready to settle down. She was the girl next door type. Settling down kind of girl. Mia reminded him of Tesla.

Whoa, not quite. Tesla was Mason's girl. She had the same grit Mia had. He remembered the way Mia had taken them into the cave and shown them what she'd found. She'd been instrumental in giving them a starting point. Now look what had happened to her – again.

He'd found her and rescued her twice, but a third time. Damn. He couldn't let those assholes hurt her. He dialed Swede and quickly gave him the update.

"Did he give a description of the truck?"

"An oversized black Ford."

"Hmmm. As in lifted?"

"No confirmation on that," Hawk said. "I'll call him back and see if we can't get a few more details." He hung up on his buddy and called Gordon back. "Do you know if there was one man in the truck or two. Was it a lifted rig or a big rig? Did it have a canopy or anything else to identify it?"

"No idea, but I know the cabbie. I'll call you back."

Hawk sat in the Jeep and waited. His mind caught on the little things Mia had done for her father. Dashing in to save him instead of taking off. Refusing to leave without him from the storehouse. Making sure Hawk was okay with carrying the extra weight. Everything she'd done had been with someone else in mind. Even at the hospital she'd wanted to leave. Said she wasn't hurt and the bed was needed for real patients. She'd been doing similar things since he'd met her.

Admirable. Made her unforgettable.

Gordon called back. "Super cab, raised, no canopy and four by. There was an off light in the left headlight. As if they lost a light and had to use whatever they could find."

"Good to know. License plate?"

"Mudded over. In fact a lot of it was pretty muddy."

"And they didn't do anything that made him question them?"

"No, just called out to her."

"Are we presuming she'd have to have known the drivers?"

"Or they had some ruse to get her attention without making her leery," Gordon said in worried tones. "She was really tired and not thinking straight."

"Damn. Okay. I'll let you know if we find anything." He ended the call and stared out the windshield blankly. His mind searched for answers.

"Nothing?" Shadow asked.

"A little bit. But we need to run the truck."

"Good luck. Trucks dominate the roads, and I swear black has got to be the most popular color."

"Maybe, but the highway patrol needs to be on the lookout."

"So, who are you calling? The sheriff?"

"Mason."

CHAPTER 11

THE TRUCK NEVER stopped. The rolling of the wheels lulled her into sleep and out of sleep and back under again. She had to go to the bathroom but she kept telling her body to forget it, that kind of relief wasn't going to happen any time soon. They'd have to stop for gas at some point unless they had a big tank in the back. From her viewpoint, she couldn't tell.

From the front came an odd rustle then sounds of food being eaten. Thankfully she wasn't offered anything. The way the wheels churned through the miles, in combination with her position, she'd have upchucked anything she tried to put down. Although a drink of water would be lovely.

But not going to happen.

She lay quiet. *Hawk, if you can hear me, please tell Dad I love him.*

She didn't know why she was talking to Hawk, then again why not, considering it was all fantasy. She could have just as easily been calling to her father. But instead she'd chosen Hawk. Why?

Because she wanted to see him again. Wanted to be held by him again. This time with affection. He confused her. Made her feel things she'd forgotten were things she'd always hoped to have. It wasn't the white picket fence dream she wanted so much as wanting that special person to be there for her. Knowing she was part of a special twosome in a world of twosomes. She wanted to wake up to the same person morning after morning and know he'd be there on the next morning too.

Foolish maybe, considering his job, but she'd rather have years with him than decades without him. And this was just stupid. Hawk didn't even know she existed. Then again not many men did.

Not a good time to reflect on her life. A good life but not one of excitement or even half interesting events.

What a waste. Sure she'd been doing more training for her Search and Rescue work, but that was nothing to what she could do. No, she'd stayed small town so she wouldn't be pushed out of her comfort zone. How was that working out for her now? She could do so much more in her field, but she'd resisted leaving Canford because it was safe.

Lord she was a fool. Hawk was a man of the world. He wasn't going to want anything to do with her. She was a mouse. And he was a predator in a good way. She'd do well to run.

Except she'd love to be pounced on. The analogy made her smile. He was so much more than she was used to. She'd love to think she was up to the challenge. She'd also love to be flippant and in control right now. It would get beaten out of her soon enough.

At that her tears started.

She tried to make them stop, but her body refused to follow orders. Instead every part of her screamed from being in the same damn position for too long. The stress and pain and panic had caught up with her although she wasn't willing to blame it on the drugs, but they'd had an effect on her too. She was a mess. She hated it.

She tried to shift her position, only she couldn't move. Why couldn't she move yet?

She hadn't felt anything for a long time, but now for some reason her body just wouldn't stop feeling. She wished it would go back to numb. It was weird but more comfortable than the screaming pain of now.

She lifted a hand and realized in shock that it moved! Not enough and not in control but whatever he'd done was wearing off.

Finally.

"How is she doing back there?"

She closed her eyes, letting her arm fall back in the position it had been in as the seats creaked with movement.

"She's the same. Out cold."

"She should be waking up soon. How hard did you knock her out?"

"Hardly. Besides, if she died we could just ditch her. So much easier."

"Not until we find out who the hell she told."

"Just the couple of guys she was with."

"Maybe, and if so, who the hell were they? No one gets away like they did. There had to be some training there. And if that's the case we need to know."

"Why, we'll be in and out and the job done before anyone realizes."

"But training means they are likely law enforcement or military."

"So? They have the gun cache so you know both are going to be brought in." He shrugged. "Makes no difference if there are one or two extra."

"But what if they saw us? The best way is in and out, but that only works if no one is waiting for us."

"True."

She heard the sound of vinyl seats as the man shifted again. She could imagine the scary dude leaning over to take a closer look. Thankfully her hair had fallen over her face so he shouldn't be able to see her eyes or the tear tracks on her cheeks.

"She's out. So until she wakes up there's nothing any of us can do."

"We'll wake her up. No worries there."

And he laughed. A laugh that let her know she wouldn't have the luxury of sleeping through whatever they had planned. They were going to get their answers no matter what.

"WE NEED A better way to track these guys."

"Mason is looking for details on the dead man, identified as Stan Slater. He's the one they killed and left behind."

"Known associates?" Shadow asked.

"Yeah, coming up on screen now."

Hawk's cell phone showed several men. He flicked through each, taking a long look to make sure he re-membered the features in case he stumbled across them. On the last one, he stopped. "This was the second guy that came with Stan."

Shadow reached out a hand for the phone. He took a long look and shook his head. "Never seen him."

"He's one of them." Hawk quickly responded to Mason, knowing he'd widen the search for this guy's associates. In the meantime he'd forward the email to Swede ahead of them.

"The more we find…"

"Aha," Hawk said as a second email came in from Mason. "The second man has an F 350."

"Good. License plate?"

"He's got one and is sending out the alert."

"Excellent." They pulled into a gas station. While Shadow filled up, Hawk walked inside. "Hey, we're tra-velling with a couple of friends but seem to have lost them, did a black F 350 come in a little while ago?"

"Maybe, a big black rig came by about an hour ago. They filled up and paid at the pump. Never came in he-re."

Hawk nodded. "That might have been them. Good to know. Two of them?"

"Yeah, looked like it. Not real friendly. I was watching, just trying to keep an eye on them like I'm supposed to, but one glared at me something fierce. Hard to believe he's got any friends."

"Yeah, he's got a chip on his shoulder a mile wide. Doesn't like people much."

"The damn brush cut makes him look military, but with that attitude. He wasn't no homeboy. Merc all the way."

Hawk stayed and chatted for a few moments longer, bought a couple of cups of coffee and walked back to the truck to tell the others.

"Good," Shadow said. They switched places so Hawk was now driving. "It's likely to be them."

Hmm. "He couldn't identify them other than a nasty visage of contempt for the general humanity at large."

"Nice. Then terrorists often do have a sense of superiority or condemnation for their fellow man. But to blow up the Golden

Gate Bridge…"

"Mason's on that. The dead man's residence is being searched right now. The bridge is being searched right now. Security detail around the clock."

"It's a long span. Easy to hide underneath and cause a lot of damage."

"True."

The conversation continued as they backed out different options and theories. An hour out of California, they stopped for gas again. This time the questions didn't offer any progress. They headed to the hotel Mason had set up. Hawk stood on the deck outside. He couldn't help but worry about Mia. Where was she?

They had to find her. And soon. These men had an agenda. But why her?

As the darkness became complete, he stood, frustration eating at him. Swede walked over. "We'll find her. She's strong. She'll do what needs to be done. She'll know we're coming."

He nodded. "We are coming. She just has to hold on."

CHAPTER 12

M IA WAS HAULED out of the truck and dumped. When her head connected with the hard ground, she saw stars. Again. Where was she? With her eyes open she could see a large warehouse, plank floor and shadows. Plenty of shadows. She let her eyes drift closed as the voices continued around her.

"We need to check in."

"I just texted them."

"Should call them instead."

"Then call them." Short disinterested. She wondered at their relationship. More business than friends. Comrades maybe. United by a cause. Blow up the Golden Gate Bridge. Just the thought of what the people in San Francisco could face in the next few days horrified her. There had to be hundreds of people on that bridge at any one time. Closer to thousands in rush hour.

Why would terrorists choose that target?

Why would they think it would make a difference? Except to make everyone hate terrorists that much more. Who won in a scenario like this? Acts of terrorisms only spread hate, fear and increased violence.

No one won. Worse, the losers counted in the thousands. Loss of innocence. Fear of what had once been normal. Of what had been comfortable.

She felt sorry for the people in the city. No one understood the dangers lurking under the surface of their seemingly easy, fun lives. It wasn't something anyone could dwell on. It was too horrible. Better to focus on the good things and let the rest go. There was too much to worry about so better to turn your back on the worry and do your best to live as well as possible.

At least that was as far as she could figure out for herself. She needed to find a level of peace with the darkness lurking outside her world.

Now in her world.

If she survived, she knew the world wouldn't be the same. How could it be? No one returned to the place they were before a horrific event. It wasn't like they could wipe it all away. As much as they might want to, they couldn't. They were forever changed by the new circumstances in their life. Just like she would be.

She'd never looked at a big black pickup like this one and not wonder if that driver was the same one who'd kidnapped her. Would she ever drive over the Golden Gate Bridge without being terrified of it blowing up beneath her wheels? And caves......
She'd had a hard time going into those damn depths before, although she'd done her best to keep it to herself. What was she going to do now? She'd have to force herself back inside.

She couldn't let other people suffer because of her failures.

"Should have dumped her in the caves."

"Might still."

She closed her eyes, a shudder running down her spine. Buried alive in a cave system that went on forever. God...what a horrible death. Not easy and it sure as hell wouldn't be quick.

"Right."

"The prick is on the way."

She froze. Who was that? And why?

"Good. He can get rid of her. She's a liability."

"Maybe. It's what it is."

"Stupid is what it is," but the voice was fading, the footsteps carrying him further away.

She wanted to roll over and ease the pain in her shoulders, but there wasn't any direction to roll. She was beside a stack of packs. Army green and stuffed with God only knew what. Her gaze landed on the knife in the back of the packs. Could she reach it? Could she use it? Without being seen?

She shifted into a sitting positions so she was leaning back against the bags. She couldn't feel the knife edge against her waist. In her mind, she reoriented herself with the layout of the bag so she could shift as needed. She'd only get one chance.

Wiggling her butt backwards until she came up against the packs, her fingers frantically searched for the knife behind her.

Finally her fingers touched something cold. She slipped the pocketknife out of the pack.

"What the hell do we have here?"

The voice stood in front of her. She froze. She'd been so focused on getting the knife, she hadn't heard him approach.

Her arm was roughly grabbed and she was lifted to her feet. Feet that could barely hold her. In fact as soon as she put her weight on them, she sagged in place.

Shit.

But her fingers still held the pocketknife. In the confusion of trying to stand, she managed to get the knife into her back pocket. Success. The same man who'd attacked her and shoved her into the truck dragged her to the far side of the warehouse. She tried to look around, but all she could see were boxes and crates. Off to the left, there were several tables full of tools. In the center was a large pallet with huge jugs of liquid, but she had no idea what they were or what they could be used for.

"Interested?" He laughed. "No worries. We might just tie you up to that bomb and make you the main at-traction."

Ice flooded her veins and she stumbled.

"Bloody hell." He pulled hard, jerking her off her feet. She tripped and went down, the fall forcing a startled cry out of her. With another hard tug, he half dragged, half shoved her into a corner and said, "You can watch from there."

She rolled onto her back and tried to catch her breath as pain radiated down every bone in her body. She wanted to sit up where she could keep watch on what they were doing, but her body still wouldn't work properly. Whatever he'd done had left a lasting impression. There was a wall a few feet away. With effort she rolled over until she was leaning up against it.

There in the shadows of the darkness, she listened to what – water close by – lapping against the wall. And she realized they were on the docks somewhere. A warehouse on the water, maybe the bay was under her. She knew they were in San Francisco from what she'd been able to figure out. The docks also made sense, but how was she to identify it further than that?

She peered between the boards and watched the water ripple below her. Amazing. She'd take her chances in the water if she could get there. Anything to get away from the men. Peering around, she realized they were busy working on something in the middle of the room. She could see stacks of small green bricks but had no clue what they were. Or indeed what the rest of the items in the warehouse were.

There had to be a way out of here. Maybe if she was ever left alone. Maybe when the prick got here. Whoever the hell that was.

A truck pulled up in the front. "About damn time he got here," one of the men muttered.

"Watch it. Don't you let him hear you say that," the other man warned. "Nothing can screw up now."

"I hear you but we're doing all the damn work."

They waited for the new arrival to join them in the warehouse. She heard his voice first. Then his face moved into view and almost laughed. He was well named. The Prick, Tom Channel. Rich asshole, and the father of the punk kid, Travis, forever hounding her at the store – and anywhere where he could catch her. She was no fool and had been avoiding him for years. Her father knew about the problem. When Tom came looking to buy the store, her father had no trouble refusing. Particularly when Tom said he'd likely give the business to his son.

That was more than her father could stand. And as she now recalled, there was talk of buying some forty acres of hillside behind his place that her father owned as well. There were a few caves in there, but so far her father had held out. She knew he could use the money – in a big way – but he didn't want to sell off the acreage.

She understood. Tom Channel hadn't.

And from the look on his face, he was looking forward to having a talk with her. She thought her memory was dredging up bits and pieces about him having a military background then going into politics. That was the thing she didn't understand. He fit the politic role perfectly. Slimy used car salesman dressed up to go to town. That part she could see in every line of his face – the military background now – that was a whole different story.

She figured if he'd actually been in the military, chances were good he'd washed out.

As in all the way out.

HAWK PACED THE room. They'd received word of a potential sighting of the truck in the city by the docks. He wanted to go down now and look for it. For her. Local police were looking for it.

More intel was coming in, but in tiny drips and drabs. And if there was one thing he wasn't good at, it was waiting.

He wanted to do *something*.

Shadow said, "The city just reported back no unusual activity."

"They can't consider the search done yet," he exclaimed. "That's a massive area."

"They aren't done but have gone through the areas that were designated as most likely." Shadow's voice was full of...well shadows. He walked with one foot in the darkness. "I've contacted a couple of guys. See if they've heard any rumors."

"If the guys are any good, they should have heard a whisper of something released. That whisper isn't going to get a happy reception. It's one thing to be part of a terrorist cell if you're not part of the community and don't care. But that bridge is a major hub. Losing it is going to make life impossible."

"The cell won't care."

"No, but anyone who hears the rumors will." And that played well into their hands. No one was going to let this happen. It could be them on the bridge.

Shadow's phone buzzed. He scrolled through the texts then

slipped a little away and called his contact.

Hawk listened with only half an ear. But something caught his attention. He turned and walked closer.

"What type of equipment?" Shadow said into the phone.

Shadow frowned, his gaze going to Hawk. "We talking C4 or chemicals?"

"You're sure about that?" Shadow asked. "Okay. We'll check it out."

"What's up?" Hawk asked when he ended the call.

"This guy saw a panel van make several deliveries to a warehouse. A forklift moved pallets of explosives out to the warehouse. He'd been casing the place beside it. He'd been inside when he thought the van was approaching, so he'd slipped out the back and into the next one. And that was when he saw them unloading, using a forklift. Said the place was set up with tables, extra lights and a lot of electrical equipment. He knows nothing about bomb equipment, but something there had his back freezing."

"Any sign of Mia," Hawk asked in a tight voice.

"He didn't mention a prisoner. Said it wasn't set up with a long term appearance, but they were comfortable as if it had been there for weeks at least."

"But no sign of a hostage?"

"I'm asking him." Shadow turned slightly away and spoke to his informant again. "What time of day and was there a woman there?"

"Early this morning and no woman." The informant's voice rose.

"Right. If it's the same group, they've taken a woman prisoner. We need to know if they still have her or if they have dumped her along the way."

Hawk's throat closed. He struggled to swallow the hard truth. But he knew it was well within the realm of possibility she'd been thrown out like garbage.

"Right." Shadow frowned. "We're going to be doing the same. Stay in touch."

He closed the phone and turned to face Hawk. "He's going to go back down and take a look."

"Is that wise?" Hawk didn't want anyone mucking up the plans. And he had no intention of listening to his orders to stay put. He was heading down there in a few minutes. He just didn't want Shadow's contact to get in the way.

"No, but he's planning to finish the job he was working on when he got sidetracked."

"Right. Of course he is." Hawk snorted. "Once a thief, always a thief."

Shadow smiled. "Yeah, but for the moment he's our thief."

"Let's go."

CHAPTER 13

T HE BLOW CAME from left field. She moaned as it cracked against her head. Again. Then the question came. Again.

"Tell us who the men are?"

She gave the same answer she'd given every other time. "I have no idea who they were."

The words never stopped. The same words came at her over and over again. How many men? Who were the men? Why these men? Were they military? What military?

Time rolled on and the pain rolled on. Nothing stopped them. Her face swelled, her lips cracked. Her tongue could barely move. Her eyes swelled shut. Her head boomed from the blows. Her shoulders were close to being dislocated from the socket. Every blow jerked her to the side. The pain radiated down her body in never-ending waves.

Hawk, where are you, she whispered in her head. *If it's not too much bother, please…help.*

She closed her eyes, willing the darkness take her.

Just as she was about to find the joy of the silence, cold water splashed in her face. She gasped and cried out in shock.

"What the hell is wrong with her?"

"No idea. Not normal. Normally the women are blubbering uncontrollably by now."

"Some kind of code of honor. Oh well. She'll break at one point."

It would be her body that would break. Actually it already had. She figured her collarbone for sure. Only the pain didn't stop there. It just radiated throughout her fingertips. She wasn't going to last much longer before she lost consciousness again.

This asshole, Tom, she'd only known one side of him. And he didn't understand the people he was working with. There was money involved and that was all he cared about.

Sad.

But, oh so damn typical. As far as she was concerned, he deserved everything he had coming to him. Did he even realize what the others were up to? How could anyone who'd fought for his country let something like this happen? Or did he have some kind of foolish concept he'd be able to stop it in time. Save the country and get kudos for his part in it all.

"How the hell is she still conscious?"

Tom walked over from the other side of the room. "Her father is the same damn type of stubborn."

She lifted her head and glared at him.

He smirked. "And the same kind of stupid."

Her defiance was short lived. She slowly lowered her head but still kept an eye on them.

"What if she doesn't actually have anything to tell us."

"Then she's useless. But she knows something, and whatever it is has to be major or else she'd have told us a long time ago."

The other men looked at each other behind his back. She'd wondered at the undercurrents. As if the others were only letting Tom believe he was the boss. She didn't get the politics in this little game they were playing, but she suspected Tom was bankrolling it, and when they were done with him, he was expendable – moneyman or not.

"It couldn't be too important."

"Whoa, hold on. We've been checking the other people in her little community she's close to. And there's a best friend. Eva Loring. Eva's brother is a SEAL."

Silence.

Her heart sinking, she was desperate not to let on that their news meant anything. If she showed by even the slightest reaction they were on to something, she'd become expendable and worse, they'd know who else to target.

"What's the chance the brother was actually there at the time?" The driver of the black truck, she thought his name was Dave, turned to Tom. "You said you checked out the men who she was with, and they were of no consequence."

"They weren't," Tom said casually. "SEALs are an overrated group of military muscles minus the brains."

Wow. Mia hoped there were SEALs listening. They'd make sure he paid for that. And what was his beef with them anyway?

"But they have connections and power we don't need. It also means that if they know Mia, they are likely to come after her."

"So?" Tom shrugged. "They are nothing."

"You're wrong," Dave said. "If you have brought them to our door…"

Tom spun to glare at Dave. "Then what? Then you'll kill them just like you've killed so many others before them. I want Gordon's land. You want your little deal here. We are already done, so it's not an issue. Dump her. See if I care. I hadn't expected you to bring her here in the first place. Once I realized you had her I wanted to know what she knew. But now…" he shrugged. "Kill her."

Dave nodded in Mia's direction, and she knew they were coming to a turning point she wasn't going to like. "Kill her yourself."

HAWK WATCHED THE scenario in the brightly lit warehouse. There were enough holes in the plank walls for anyone to see inside. And what he saw was making him crazy. Mia was there but he was behind her. She'd been tied to a chair where she sat, her head slumped to the side as if she were unconscious. Blood dripped to the floor. His jaw clenched. They'd pay for hurting her.

"That's what you guys are here for," the man in jeans and suit jacket said.

Hawk could see his face but didn't recognize him. Although he had to be from Canford if he was trying to acquire Gordon's land.

"You're not in for the cause. Just your own cause."

"Remember who paid for all this." Tom narrowed his gaze, his hands going to his hips.

Hawk watched the expressions roll across the men's faces as they wiggled within their power hierarchy. He wondered if the "boss" had any idea he wasn't anything close to being a boss. That he was expendable and likely here and now.

"She can identify you as well, so you'll have to kill her. She's your problem."

Hawk's gaze caught on the large table on the left with a tangle of electrical cables and connectors. Timers. Shit. They needed a team here. Now. But Mia didn't have the time. He slid down the long wall looking for another peephole.

From the new position, his gaze swept the room. And landed on Mia's face.

God damn it.

She'd been pulverized.

Why? She didn't know anything.

"She was supposed to tell us who she was with. Who rescued her? Who we were up against?"

"Well, she didn't. Now she's past the point of being able to. So get rid of her."

They were dead. That was all there was to it. He didn't give a damn about protocol and procedure and justice. These men had beaten an innocent women into hamburger. He was going to take them out. He'd do it for any woman, that it was Mia? Sweet gentle, brave Mia who hadn't given them up…made his blood boil.

From all the times he'd met her, watched her with her father, listened to his own sister go on and on about her best friend, Hawk understood she was so damn afraid of not being good enough, that she took special care to be the best she could be. To learn more to help out. To be so much better because she was afraid she was so far away from decent. In truth, she was much better than everyone. Always had been. He'd watched her stop to help a crying child, carry groceries for an older man. She was always there, always around. Always in the background.

Damn.

Where was Shadow? Being a shadow, of course was something he was damn good at. Going unseen in the most dangerous places. He caught a movement from the corner of his eye and realized Shadow was inside the warehouse. Shit. He shifted so he could watch the others, see if they noticed his presence. But they were caught in their own power-play.

As he watched, the other man opened up the back of the van parked to the left. Hell. The van was full. The man called to someone and yet a fourth male came over and helped load up boxes. From his position, Hawk couldn't see enough to be useful. He ran down the side of the building. Where had Shadow gone? He couldn't see him. As the two men finished loading the van, they called over to the arguing men. "Loaded."

One of the two men who'd been loading walked to the boss, pulled out a gun and shot him in the head.

He crumpled silently to the floor.

"About damn time. Stupid ass. You could have done that an hour ago and saved me the stress."

"He's an idiot. We had to check he'd sent the last payment. We've just got confirmation that the money is in the bank."

Shit. Hawk knew that meant they had money and that meant a hell of a lot of freedom.

"And her?"

"Toss her into the river. Should have shot her in the damn hospital parking lot. Waste of time and energy. Fix the mistake."

And he turned back to loading more things into the van.

"We shouldn't throw them both into the river at the same time. The cops will connect the two incidents."

The other men nodded. "Get rid of the prick," he sniggered. "Keep her until morning. We'll throw her out tomorrow."

Like a sack of garbage. Hawk struggled to contain the rage boiling through his blood. She had more bravery than any of these assholes. There's no way he was letting anything else happen to her.

She wasn't going to die like this.

"Not going to happen." Hawk slipped around to the side where the men were busy dragging the boss man to the far back. He could see a small trap door that opened to the water below.

"Weigh him down good. He can't pop up until we're long gone."

"We can leave him here if you want. He'll hold for half a day."

"No, that's just going to bring in the rats. We don't need that. Get rid of the body, just make sure it doesn't show until we're out of the country."

Out of the country? Hawk quickly sent a text to Mason. As he lifted his gaze, the van drove away. He raced to the side to catch the license plate, but it wasn't visible. He took a picture anyway and sent it on. They needed to track that vehicle.

He'd seen four men. One was gone, possibly two. That left two men behind. And Mia.

Those were his kind of odds.

CHAPTER 14

THE DARKNESS RIPPLED around her. She couldn't think. Her mind flooded in a sea of darkness, and she just wanted this to be over. She was glad she'd spent time with her father before leaving. At least he'd be okay. Eva would miss her, but she'd be fine. No one else would know or care.

Now that the end was here, she was surprisingly good with it.

"Mia?"

The soft voice was warm against her ear. She was dead then. 'Cause that was Hawk's voice. So sweet to take that across the great divide with her. Unless...her heart froze.

Unless he was dead too.

Moving her lips as little as possible, she whispered, "Are you dead too?"

"No. I'm not. Neither are you."

"Yes, I am." She reached up and stroked his beautiful face. "If you're with me, I am. You're too pretty to be with me any other way."

He shook his head. "You're not making sense. Don't try to talk. You're hurt. We're getting you some help."

"Help would be good. I do like to help."

"No, we are getting help for you," he stressed. "Not for you to help."

She struggled to sort through the crazy confusion in her head. "Sorry, I'm not much good right now. They caught me," she said in low tones. "I didn't tell them anything."

"What is she saying?" Shadow whispered beside them. "I can't hear what she said."

"You shouldn't be here," she mumbled in a louder voice. "They'll come after you."

"Good," Hawk said. "Let them try." He was behind her now, she could feel anger. She didn't understand.

"You have to leave. You'll get hurt."

Her arms suddenly fell forward as if the ties had been cut. She cried out. But he had already cut the ties around her ankles and was swinging her up into his arms. She shuddered as her body still managed to react to the new position. To her nerves screaming as they bolted in awareness again.

"Easy. We're getting you out of here."

She closed her eyes. "Forget about me. Stop them. They are going to blow up the bridge."

"We'll stop them. You however, do matter. Get that into your head."

She tried to smile, but her mouth hurt too much to move more than a wiggle.

"Don't move, it's making things worse."

"Watch out for the men," she whispered. "Don't want them to get you."

"We already took them out. They won't be hurting anyone again." He looked down at her and smiled. "How about you let someone else handle things for a while."

He moved her gently into a vehicle of some kind. "I promise.

Those two aren't coming back ever again."

There were sounds of an ambulance in the distance. Cops. Relief filled her. "Did you call them?"

"Yeah, we have a few dead men here to cart away and one heroine to save."

"Not me. Not heroine material."

Warm lips pressed against her forehead. "Definitely heroine material."

People swarmed toward them.

She was laid down on a bed of some sort. "I'm fine. I just need to go to sleep for a while," she protested sleepily.

"When the doctor says you're fine then you can sleep, but in the meantime…"

Suddenly she was surrounded by people and noise. It was too much to sort out. A warm blanket was spread over her then straps went over top, and she sank into a peaceful oblivion.

As she went under, she reached out and grabbed for his hand. "Thank you."

"TAKE GOOD CARE of her," Hawk ordered.

The ambulance driver nodded as he loaded Mia into the back of the ambulance. "She's lucky to be alive."

"I know." Hawk glared at the chaos around him. The hunt was on for the van, but this place would be active all night with three dead men behind him. That left one driver to hunt down.

Shadow had kept out of the limelight. Now he approached Hawk. "You ready to move out?"

"Yeah." He didn't move though as he stared at the ambulance's rearview lights disappearing into the distance. "Do we have eyes on the van?"

"Not yet." Shadow was searching through his messages. "This place will garner us a lot of useable in-formation."

"Not fast enough. That bomb is potentially ready to go." Still he couldn't pull himself away from where she'd been. The lights of the ambulance were long gone. Still, he stood there.

"Mason has a couple of leads. Come on."

He spun to look at Shadow. "I'm going to go to the hospital. See how she is."

Shadow nodded. "I'll recon with Swede and swing by and pick you up."

Getting away took a little longer than Hawk was prepared for. Still, he made it in just over a half hour to find the hospital teeming with bodies from a multi car pileup. It took a few moments for him to flag down a nurse to tell him where Mia had been taken only to find out she wasn't at that hospital at all.

Worried, he raced out to the parking lot and called Shadow. "She's not here."

"Taken to a different hospital?" Shadow questioned. "If there's a bad car accident, that's possible."

"Damn well better be. If we handed her over to the ass-holes..."

"There's no reason for them to take her now. They'd have just killed her on the spot."

He knew that. He was already in his Jeep driving toward the second hospital. "Call and see if she's there."

"On it."

He was on the main drag, only blocks from the second hos-pital when Shadow called back. "She's there."

"Good." He pulled up to the front and hopped out. He

raced inside. And found her. She was in the first examining room. A nurse hovered over her.

"Hey, what are you doing here?" Mia said, trying to sit up. "You're supposed to be chasing bad guys."

"We are but I needed to know how badly hurt you are."

"Not," she murmured.

Hawk caught the nurse's gaze and she smiled. "We're sending her for X-rays soon then we'll know for sure."

Right. He could have just called. But he'd needed to see her again. He bent down and whispered, "I might have to leave, but you call me if you need anything. You got that?"

Surprise lit her face. She murmured, "Thanks. But you go save the world."

He grinned. "Will do. You save yourself, you hear me. Make sure you are healing by the time I get back."

She stared at him, her gaze dark, fathomless. "*Will* you be back?"

He leaned over and kissed her. "I will."

And he left.

CHAPTER 15

THE X-RAYS CLINCHED it. She was booked in the hospital and told to expect her stay to last for a few days. Now that she was in bed, medication pulsing through her veins, clean sheets and lots of water, all she wanted to do was sleep.

But her mind wouldn't shut down. She wanted to go home. At least talk to her father. Let him know she was alive.

Did she have a cell phone any longer? The nurse walked in just then and she asked her.

"There is a phone. And your knife. They're in a bag for you." The nurse smiled at her. "I'll put them on the side table."

"No, bring it please. It's not mine, it's from the kidnappers."

With a look of surprise the nurse hurried to a cupboard on the side and returned a few minutes later with both items. As much as she wanted to call her father, it was the knife that interested her. She turned it over in her hands. And found the initials JF on the top corner. She didn't know if that would help anyone or not. Initials weren't terribly helpful. Besides, they already knew what the plan was. They needed to identify the assholes involved, but the initials weren't going to help that much. Especially as he might have taken it off someone else. She opened the knife and pulled the blade all the way out. It was big and deadly sharp. A hunting knife. With dried blood in the hinge. Human or animal?

She picked up her phone and called Hawk. "Not sure it makes any difference, but I managed to steal a knife from one of the guy's packs. I hadn't had an opportunity to use it, but it was in my pocket at the hospital here. It's got blood on it and the initials JF on the outside."

"I'll get someone to collect it. Keep it safe until they get there." His voice deepened. "And you stay safe. Remember, we got this."

She laughed as she hung up. "Yeah, he's got this."

With that happy thought, she dialed her father. "Dad?"

"Jesus, Mia, are you okay?"

"I am now," and she burst into tears. Silly. After a few moments she managed to get a hold of herself and explain what happened.

"Oh my Lord. I'm so sorry baby. I should never have let Gerry back into our lives."

"That might not have changed anything." She told him about Tom wanting to buy the land. "Dad, I think there has to be a reason why he's so adamant about the land."

"It's full of caves, but I have no idea why they'd care. I haven't been down there in years. Last time wasn't all that pleasant, so I just avoided it after that. Hell, it's closer to fifteen years since I explored that area."

"Maybe it's full of guns too."

"I doubt it. He was twisted and power hungry, but he was more money hungry."

"Any chance of precious metals or minerals?"

"No idea. Honestly, he wasn't all there with his get rich schemes. Now sure, he's wealthy and all that, but it's old family money. No idea if any of his ideas ever worked out."

"Doesn't matter now. He's dead. His son might not even know the news yet." She didn't relish seeing him again. He'd lost his father and that had to hurt. She was grateful to have her father with her still. She'd come so close to losing him several times lately.

"He will soon enough. I'm being released. Got to go back to the store and see how much damage has been done while no one has been there."

"The place has likely been cleaned out."

"Maybe it should stay that way. It just might be time to sell it. Too bad the only one who wanted to buy it is now dead."

She understood how he felt. Still he didn't sound happy about his decision. And she wanted him to be happy. "You don't have to make a decision now." She shifted in the bed. "Wait until you get there and see how you feel."

A cop came to her doorway and looked around. She had a room to herself for which she was grateful, and it was as nice as it was unexpected.

"Sorry, someone is here. I'll call you back later."

And she hung up her phone before calling to the young man. "Hi, were you looking for this?"

She held up the knife. "Hawk said he'd send someone to collect it."

"That would be me."

"Do you know Hawk well or are you part of the local force and just the errand boy?" she said with a smile.

"Hawk," he said with a laugh. "Who's he?"

"Oh just the SEAL bringing this whole operation down." She handed it over. "Take good care of it. It belongs to one of the kidnappers. I stole it from them." She yawned. "Sorry, the pain killers are really knocking me out. Good thing you came now. I'll be asleep in a few minutes."

He gave her a big wide mouthed smile. "Yeah, you will."

HAWK STARED DOWN at the map in front of him. An old engineer's map of the bridge and the footings as it had been originally built was fascinating reading. And left too many opportunities for massive damage from bombs laid at the right location.

It's not something bridges were ever designed against. The span was too great. The traffic too heavy. No one wanted to make the call to shut down the main artery on rumors. No one wanted to take the fall if this was found to be a hoax.

He knew it wasn't a hoax, but he wasn't sure many people were listening. Except his team. Mason was pulling more magic to help keep them in the middle of things. None of it mattered to him. He was after the men before the bomb was placed in their location. In order to do that he had to figure out where the most likely place was to set off the bomb for maximum damage. From a single entry position because that was simpler and faster than multiple detonations. That meant it had to be big enough and he wasn't sure what he'd caught a glimpse of was big enough. They had to consider multiple strike points.

And that meant more vehicles, more men…and more places where they'd be vulnerable.

While the men behind him argued, he and Shadow, with Swede running the computer searches on the terrorists, plotted the best route as if they were planning to take the bridge down themselves.

It was always easier to stop an op if you understood the way the enemy was planning to go.

"I don't know. It would have to be too damn big. It's not going to blow downward, it will blow upward. Some damage but minor in the scheme of things," Shadow said. His finger stabbed the map at the far entrance. "The foundations here are massive. Again the number of bombs, the types, the size...I don't know..." He shook his head. "I'm not liking this at all."

"I know what I'd do," Hawk announced. "Underwater and take out the supports. This would give them the advantage of working under the cover of the water."

Swede stood up and walked over to the map. "That would be a hell of a plan."

"Access off what, a ferry? Those are big vans and now with the type of cargo they are carrying – heavy."

"How about a barge or better yet an older fishing vessel? The bay is full of those," Hawk said, staring at the paper, but in his mind he could see the water churning in front of him. "A large fishing boat is a common site, big enough to handle the weight."

"A barge is too unwieldy," Shadow said. "And they don't have power of their own. A fishing boat would work but would have a hard time coming into dock in this area."

"True, but a tugboat would be able to go back and forth easily enough. They also anchor outside and have a powerboat for coming to shore. No one would consider either option odd."

His phone rang. He pulled it out, read the number and smiled. "Hey Gordon, you home now, causing trou-ble?"

"Mia's gone missing again. She was checked out, X-rayed and booked into a room and given pain meds for the beating she took. The nurse went back in to check on her and she's gone. Not her clothes or her shoes, just her. Gone without a trace."

His voice broke as he said the next words. "They've got her. They won't let her live this time."

Hawk spun to stare at his friends, then back at the task force behind them. He took a deep breath, then in as calm and controlled a voice as he could muster, he said, "Gordon, I'm going to call you right back."

And he hung up. With his chest pounding and panic stirring his blood to action, he said tersely, "Mia's gone. No sign of her. Hospital bed empty. Her clothes left behind."

The men's gazes narrowed to slits.

"They took her?" Shadow asked incredulously. "Why?"

The television blared an alert. "We've just been given a message. A terrorist group is claiming to have a captive that they are going to blow up along with the cargo terminals if their demands aren't met."

"Does that answer the question?" Swede asked as the newcaster droned on behind them.

There on the television, obviously drugged and still in her hospital gown, face bruised and bloody already, yet hanging from a post, was Mia.

"Dear God," Hawk whispered. "What have they done to her?"

CHAPTER 16

S HE WAS AN idiot. That's all there was to it. She was a stupid fool. Maybe the morphine was responsible for her loose tongue. She'd suffered through the asshole's torture and finally she was safe – and blurted out the first thing that came to her head when she saw the young cop. Only he wasn't a cop. But she hadn't known until he'd picked up the knife and pocketed it with a "thanks for that. My daddy gave me that knife. I really didn't want to lose it."

He'd smirked and said, "Very naughty of you, but I do like spirit in a woman. Too bad there's no time for us to get to know each other. But the guys have figured out a good use for you. Especially now." His smile had made her blood run cold.

And she'd lost consciousness. She didn't know if he'd hit her, drugged her, or something else, but that was the last thing she remembered.

Now she was cold, scared and hurting like she hadn't hurt before. She really could use more painkillers. Why were they after her again? She'd done nothing, knew nothing. She had no money or prestige or power.

There was no reason to keep coming after her.

And she'd really like to go home now, please.

Then they'd shoved the camera in her face for the second

time. She stared into it and hoped Hawk was watching. She was on an old fishing boat of some kind but she had no idea where. Likely under the damn bridge they were all talking about. She was apparently going to be attached to the bomb. Like really. When she decided to have a shitty day, she had a *really* shitty day.

Facing the camera, she moved her fingers slightly. She needed to get a message out, but how? She didn't know any secret codes. And had no freedom of movement. She stared at the camera when told too and read the words they gave her to read. It was all lies. They weren't going to let her go.

She stared into the camera and whispered, "Sorry Hawk." As the cameras were shutting off, she mouthed, "Fishing boat."

And unbelievably they didn't seem to notice. Or at least they didn't show her if they had. She dropped her head. She was strapped against the wall, her hands in handcuffs with a small ledge where her feet rested so her arms weren't taking all her weight. It could be worse, she knew that. But it was hard to remember such a small element.

There was nothing to do but wait. An old phrase of her father's came rushing into her mind. When all else fails, remember who you love.

Tears clogged her eyes. She missed him.

Would she ever see him again? Would she see Hawk again? She understood they were both doing what they could. And she knew what her job was. To stay alive.

MASON WALKED INTO the task force and immediately felt the bristling of the other men. They could damn well get over it. He understood Hawk's message even if Hawk hadn't.

This woman was important to him. He'd even seen her apology to Hawk on her thirty-second spotlight and damn it that sounded like his own loving partner. She'd have done the same thing. Funny, the guys and him had been with more women than they could count, but it was a woman like his own and now Hawk's that stopped them in their tracks.

And speaking of which, he saw Hawk pacing in front of a map and arguing logistics with Swede. Good. He'd brought Cooper with him too. He ignored the task force and walked to his men.

Hawk stopped in his tracks, and a look of relief washed over him. "Damn it's good to see you."

"Did you get her message?" Mason asked.

Hawk frowned. "Her damn apology? That girl would tell us to forget about her and to stop the bombing."

"Smart girl," Mason said calmly. "And you know we'd all say the same thing."

The other men slowly straightened as they realized the truth of his words. "Damn. He's right. She's one of us."

"Except she's a captive."

"And you know what that means – we aren't leaving without her," Mason said.

The others grinned. "Now we're talking."

Hawk ran his fingers through his hair. "She's something, isn't she?"

"She is and now she's our something and we take care of our own." He turned to study the map. "You guys saw her say 'fishing boat' at the very end, right?"

They bolted toward him. "No, we didn't."

He stared open-mouthed at them. "Really? The news cast I watched had the camera rolling as it moved away from her, she leaned her head to the side and mouthed 'fishing boat.'"

The others all shook their heads. Hawk said, "The version we saw didn't show her head leaning to the side at all. Damn." Hawk spun and walked to the map. "I said a large fishing boat would be the best way to transport the bomb to the underwater footings."

"So let's get the equipment we need." Mason smiled. "Looks like we'll get a chance to go swimming after all."

Getting the equipment took a little longer than they'd expected. Thankfully they didn't have to rely on the task force for the supplies. The task force wasn't on the same side of the shipping vessel that his team was, and Port Authority wasn't interested in having the docks searched at all. Also shutting things down for a few hours was impossible apparently. The task force was taking the stance that the bombs would be delivered by vehicle so they wanted the authorities to focus on those access points and stay the hell away from the docks.

That worked for Hawk. While the task force was doing that, they wouldn't be getting in the SEALs' way.

SEALs preferred to work alone and do things the way they needed, to get them done. And right now they had to find Mia. They packed up their gear and left the task force to themselves.

Outside they split up into the vehicles and drove to the docks. They were going to need intel.

"Shadow, what about your one source? Any chance he'd be able to find out about Mia?"

"He's already out there looking. I've got a couple more looking too. But I want to go down myself. Not at the same spot but up on the north side of the bridge."

Hawk nodded. "Any particular reason?"

"Yeah, it's where I'd go in."

That was good enough for him. Mason drove to the area in question and parked.

The sky was quiet. At peace. At the break of a new day. He'd taken several power naps to keep up his focus strength. As he walked around the truck and stared at the water, he had to wonder what this new day was going to bring.

Shadow pointed out the ships already working the water. There were tankers waiting to load and others waiting to unload. Dozens of sailboats bobbed in the small crests brought on by the cool wind drifting across the water.

It would be cold for Mia if she was out there. On camera she hadn't been wearing enough to keep the icy wind at bay, just a hospital gown and not much else. If she was outside, cold was going to be a major factor.

Shadow pointed out to the bay. There were several ships anchored at the mouth. Smaller watercraft bobbed around them. He studied the footings above the water and the access points from where they stood. Only two major supports, so that was where the bombs would need to be.

Easy. No guess work there.

Too easy in fact.

There were no vehicles, ships or people that they could see at the closest pylon. It looked calm and tranquil. But the water seethed around the base from the wind.

His phone beeped. "Dane has several longshoremen friends. There're rumors of some unusual cargo at the Oakland cargo facilities."

"Where?" Shadow asked. "We need more. That area is huge. Which pier for a start. And what ships are docked on that pier. Then we need the call number of the ship, so we can find it and track its movement. Might be nothing but we'll have to check them all."

"Dane also says," Hawk paused as he read the incoming text, "no woman was seen, but a body was possibly sighted." His heart dropped. "Shit. Shit. Shit."

"Easy. She's been unconscious since they hauled her out of the hospital – no way she'd have gone if she wasn't – that means a body to most people. They'd have seen her being brought in to wherever they took the video."

"Right." It had better be. She didn't deserve this shit. She'd been involved earlier because of her father, but now...now she was there because of him.

"We'll get her. Hold tight to that thought. We. Will. Get. Her." Shadow's voice was both reassuringly hard and equally pissed. That was how Hawk felt.

"Let's get down to where 'the body' was sighted. We don't want her out on the water if we can save her before that happens."

"Does she swim?" Swede asked.

"No idea."

"Well, I hope she understands water rescues because chances are good we're going to be doing one," Shadow said.

They returned to the truck as word came she'd been seen at the Seventh Street Terminal at the Port of Oakland container handling facility. And nothing clearer than that. But men were looking everywhere there for her.

Only it was massive, damn near a city in itself. Full of places she could be stashed until needed for further media frenzy moments.

Not good enough.

Hawk wanted to make sure that after all the rescues she'd participated in – someone would be there to rescue her.

CHAPTER 17

NOW WHERE WAS she? Mia could feel the rocking motion that said water. So likely she was still on the same fishing boat. Where? And why? She didn't want to be a damn prisoner again, but that was exactly what she was.

There were two men with her that she could see. They'd loaded her into a van earlier, but she'd succumbed to the cold and the rest of the drugs still coursing through her system and passed out. Now awake again, she was numb from the lack of clothing. Why couldn't they have given her a blanket at least? She knew they planned to kill her but still...

"Can I have a blanket please?" she politely asked the first man.

He ignored her.

She asked again, he ignored her again.

Great.

She turned to the second man and asked him. He looked up, saw her speaking and responded in a spate of something she didn't understand. The meaning was clear though. No, she couldn't have a blanket. She curled up into a ball and tried to hold her fears back. She refused to be a milksop. Not now.

But damn that cold was sapping her strength, both physically and mentally.

Her father had played games with her when she was younger and bored. Now she tried to keep her mind active by replaying the same games. Something about finding a country starting with the last letter in a country name. She quickly ran through as many as she could to keep her mind off the problems. Yet at the same time she had to keep considering what choices she had. Surely there was something she could do. Stay quiet and low key, don't do anything to bring up their ire and wait it out. Take the opportunity and run if she could. She was a strong swimmer. Although the bay, tired and injured as she was, might be more than she could do. But then again, her choices were limited.

She had to be ready when opportunity knocked.

And in whatever form it arrived.

If that meant going for a dunk in the bay then she'd better be ready. Besides, she'd take that over being blown to shit by a bomb any day.

Especially if it was going to be done publicly. She'd had enough nightmares. She didn't want to be the cause of more for someone else.

Besides, public executions were icky.

She grinned. At least she still had her sense of humor.

If nothing else, she could keep her head up. And stay alive.

She needed to give Hawk time to rescue her.

THE DOCKS TEEMED with life. But they had to consider not just commercial shipping but private boats that could be big enough to do the job. It was going to be impossible to track everyone.

Swede came up behind them and walked past as if not seeing them. He walked ahead a few yards then slowly cut to the left.

Hawk and Shadow followed.

"Why the Golden Gate? Why not the Oakland Bay Bridge?"

"Why any bridge? To send a message. Which bridge do you think of when you think of San Francisco?"

"Golden Gate." Shadow shook his head. "It's the iconic nature they want to blow up. The American symbolism, not the actual bridge."

"Terrorists get both in this case."

They took precious hours to walk the docks, pulling in necessary information and asking the questions that needed to be asked. It was when they were just about ready to go back to the base that one man sidled up to them.

"Heard you were asking about a woman in a hospital gown."

Hawk frowned at him. "Maybe, what's it to you?"

"More like what's it worth to you." He smiled, showing a missing front tooth. "If it's not worth anything, then it's nothing to me."

And wasn't that the truth. Did no one do anything to help others anymore?

Shadow slid forward.

The man slid back, then narrowed his gaze. "How much?"

"Tell us first then we'll decide."

He snorted. "And then you take off, without paying."

Shadow slid a half step forward.

"Shit." The toothless man backed off slightly. "I saw them carry her onto a tugboat."

"A tugboat?" Hawk froze, his mind spinning on the possibilities. A tugboat worked if they were taking out a different watercraft of some kind. Tugboats were a dime a dozen here and were a major part of the city. No one would question a tugboat's movement. They damn near ran the place. Although it could be the one vehicle they were using to move bombs, but that wasn't likely – was it? He pondered the logistics and size.

"How do you know it was her?" Shadow asked, that ever present threat in his voice slightly elevated.

"She was in the damn hospital gown. Poor thing. She didn't look conscious. I saw her on the tele too. They're going to blow her up and that's not good."

"No, it's not." Hawk thought about it a moment longer then said, "Can you identify the tugboat?"

He snorted. "There are thousands of them here."

"So you can't add anything to the little bit you told us," Shadow said in disgust. "How about where the tugboat was headed?"

"Hey, I didn't say that. First off there were two men who took her on board. A third man was driving the van. No, I didn't recognize any of them, but they were olive skinned and dark haired. All younger."

"How young?"

And the questions fired in a volley as they tried to draw out as much information as they could get from him. When he'd been paid and walked away, the two men stared at each other then broke into a run heading to where the tugboat had docked. The informant hadn't seen where it had gone except out into the harbor, and that could mean anything. But he'd given them a few identifying marks.

If they could identify that boat, they might identify where Mia had been taken. That the van was still driving around was worrisome. Not that it would help, he knew. If they were smart enough to pull this off, they were smart enough to have exchanged license plates with a different vehicle. It was a simple switch and done all the time.

At the docks they walked through the heavy winds that blew water from the ocean, soaking them instantly. Hawk stared out at the ships in the Bay. There were an easy dozen. Mostly carrying shipping containers but it wouldn't be hard to smuggle Mia aboard if they were crew members. And then again they'd likely not trust anyone and wouldn't want to be seen with her. So a private place was more likely.

His gaze caught the fishing boats riding the waves in the water. Tiny beside the container ships but some were certainly big enough to get the job done.

That meant there were more options to look at and not enough time.

At least for the moment. They could take a different escape route. Particularly if there were just a couple of them. Depending on the terrorists, it was also likely they had no plans to escape. Suicide bombings were common. Sad. Deadly. There wasn't anything new to be found except to keep watch on this place and get eyes on the water.

They had the gear ready to go and were on their own small water craft within two hours. This time there were five of them.

Hawk stared across the water, terrified of where Mia could be. There'd been no other broadcasts, but the media wouldn't leave it alone. They wanted to know who the mystery woman was, and why she'd been targeted.

It wouldn't be long before they put all the information together and found Gordon. If he stayed quiet, it might help, but now that he knew what was happening to his daughter…well, no one would blame him for doing what he thought was right.

If he thought it would save Mia, he'd do anything he could. And so would Hawk.

"Hawk, we've picked up a couple of old fishing vessels by the bridge."

"I'm coming."

CHAPTER 18

L ORD, SHE WAS cold. Her toes had turned gray and her skin had an odd purple cast to it. The terrorists didn't care about her health, she was dead already as far as they were concerned. If she was going to die anyway, she wanted to die warm. She also had to go to the bathroom.

As in now.

She tried to straighten but her arms wouldn't shift. She was no longer up against the wall. She'd been dragged to a corner and left alone. After she'd done the presentation on camera they didn't care. With her arms still tied but no longer behind her, she hugged her knees tight against the cold. A blanket, something to ward against catching a chill would be lovely. Too late. She figured. She was already frozen and injured and couldn't imagine her body having much left in the way of defenses.

One man walked closer and studied her with dark eyes.

She stared back. No longer afraid and no longer worried. She'd either live or die today. All she wanted at the moment was a bathroom and to get warm.

"Stand up." He barked the orders in a thick accented voice that took her a moment to understand. When she did, she scrambled to her feet and swayed in place.

"I need a bathroom."

He nodded. "Come with me."

And he walked out. She stumbled behind, but her feet were thick planks and not interested in following her orders. She managed to hang onto the wall and make her way. Out into some kind of hallway, the stench almost making her retch, he pushed her toward what she assumed passed for a toilet. He stood outside and waited.

She took care of business quickly. It was her first chance to move in hours and her first opportunity for an escape, but with her body functioning in slow motion she wasn't sure what she could do. But time was running out. She wracked her brain, trying to create a plan.

Another voice called out. Her captor responded in a language she didn't recognize. He turned away slightly, and she heard footsteps recede. Quickly she straightened her underwear and spun around, frantic to find a weapon of some kind.

There were shouts up deck.

With no window to look out, she couldn't see what the disturbance was. There were several blankets shoved in a corner. One was wet, but they were both better than nothing. She grabbed them and wrapped up well, her body reaching in relief for the heat. There were also old socks. She slipped them on, almost moaning in delight as her toes had a cloth barrier between them and the plank floor. There was a kitchen of sorts in the big room, maybe an old converted houseboat or fishing boat. Which would make sense. She vaguely remembered a smaller boat first, a tugboat, maybe. Then being transferred here.

There was no way to see outside from where she stood and no way to send a message. But could she slip away in the confusion? Hide? She had to try.

She did a fast search of the room, looking for anything helpful, and found a small piece of copper wire. She studied it and
wrapped it around her wrist to keep it safe.

She retraced her steps to the bathroom and the door to the
hallway. She opened it carefully.

And came face to face with a wired...something.

Running feet pounded overhead and more voices. Good, she
hoped the boats were being boarded. Preferably by the Coast
Guard. She slipped to the stairs and stared up. Could she make it
up there without being seen?

Determined to try, she crept higher. There were six steps.
She crouched lower the higher she went.

"What the fuck are you doing?"

She ducked, hoping the yelling hadn't been directed at her.

There appeared to be more people on board now. Why?
What the hell was going on?

She poked her head above the deck and took a quick look
around. It was more like an old fishing boat. The men were
behind her and waving their arms and doing lots of shouting.
Good.

She'd take any distraction she could. She focused on the
rowboat tied to the railing not six feet from her. If she could
make it there...

It was raining out. And they appeared to be in the middle of
the Bay. Miles from shore. And miles from any other boat. She
knew death was certain on board. Was it also certain in the
water?

She ran to the rowboat and ducked down beside it. She
peered over the railing. The water churned in a mad foaming
wash against the hull. She studied the rowboat hangers. There

was some kind of hydraulic system to release it. The men had guns. If she wanted a quiet escape then a rowboat wasn't it. They'd kill her before she got the rowboat to the lowered position.

A quick glance showed the men still arguing.

There really was no choice. She ditched the blanket, knowing it was only going to drag her down, and crawled through the railing. With one last thought of Hawk, she grabbed the life preserver clinging to the side of the boat and snatched the blanket up again, to hide the bright white and red colors. She needed it to stay afloat but didn't want to let them know where she was. The waves were going to take her several yards away in seconds. Out a few minutes and it wouldn't matter, she'd be long gone.

Just as she was set to jump as far off to the side as she could, the *wap wap wap* of a helicopter sounded overhead.

She waved up to it, swore she saw someone wave back and jumped.

"IS THAT HER?" Shadow pointed to the far distance and a blob of green behind a lifeboat.

Hawk stared, snatched up the binoculars and adjusted them. "It is her."

He quickly assessed the problem and what she was up to. "Crap, she's going to jump."

"She does realize she's likely to drown in this storm."

"I'm sure she's thinking that she'd rather drown than stay with them."

"If she's thinking at all."

And Hawk knew that was likely the real answer. She was reacting. She wanted to save herself and was doing what she could. He had to admire she was functioning at all. Then he watched, his heart in his throat as several men pointed in her direction. She couldn't see them from where she was hiding, but her instinct was sound. She wrapped her arms around something large and dark and jumped off as he watched.

The men on board raced to the railing.

"Shit."

He sent word to the pilot who immediately swerved the angle and flew toward the boat and the woman floundering in the water. The distance between the fishing boat and the woman widened quickly. Getting her to safety was the priority.

Hawk dumped his gear and moved to the edge of the helicopter. He'd jump in as soon as they were close. She wasn't going to swim far in this cold water. And he figured she'd be too cold to climb out herself.

A shot rang out just missing his head. The helicopter veered to the side.

"No," he yelled. "Let me off first."

"Easy." Shadow shifted position, a weapon in his hand. "We're too far away to take out the shooter. Need the rifles." And he was already up and running to the back of the helicopter.

"This is a reconnaissance mission, we didn't come loaded for bear," the pilot shouted back.

"I'm not leaving without her," Hawk snapped. Other watercraft were on their way. If the helicopter was forced to return, the two of them wouldn't need to be in the water for long.

The helicopter swung around for another attempt to get closer to Mia. The men were standing on deck, milling around uncertainly. If they opened fire on the helicopter, they would be taken out immediately. He couldn't think about that. He stayed focused on Mia. The helicopter swung in closer. Hawk was all set with Shadow back at his side, prepared to take out a shooter if they were under attack. With Mia drifting further away from the boat, Hawk jumped into the water.

Braced for the cold he sank deep then he kicked up strong. From under the waves he could see Mia about twenty feet from him. His jump appeared to have sent her rocking further away. Good. He surfaced and reached her within minutes. She was stretched out across something that he realized when he got closer was a life preserver. He wrapped an around her.

"Mia?" he called in a loud voice. "It's Hawk. I'm going to get you to safety. Hold on."

She lifted her face and stared at him. His heart swelled in pain. Her face, already ravaged by the beating, hadn't taken well to the saltwater. She reached out a hand to stroke his face. Then she started to cry.

He held her close. Thank God they'd found her. She wouldn't have survived long out in the Bay. "It's okay. I've got you."

He signaled up to Shadow. The rope harness dropped down. He quickly hooked the two of them up. Shadow called from up above and pointed behind them. Hawk looked around. The boat was motoring away. Too bad it wasn't going to get very far. As long as he rescued Mia he didn't give a damn what the bastards did. He'd be back for them soon enough. They could run – they wouldn't be able to hide.

At his okay, Shadow started the winch system to haul them both up.

Mia hung limp against him. Shivers rippled over her body, and her skin tone was grey ugly paste. Now she had to combat hypothermia on top of everything else.

"Hold on Mia. Hold on."

But she'd closed her eyes and never responded.

Then they were in the helicopter and racing her back to the medical center.

CHAPTER 19

M IA WOKE TO heat, blessed comforting heat. Maybe she was on fire. She'd been so cold before, now she burned with pain. The numbness might have been a blessing because along with her body waking up from the cold, the damaged parts were waking up too. And she hurt.

She huddled under the covers, loathe to open her eyes and see where she was. Thoughts of being home safe and sound never entered her mind. As if that were too far a stretch of the truth. But she needed to know. She peeked under her lashes. White everywhere. The sheets, the pillow against her face, the curtains around her. A hospital? Or something else? She couldn't tell. But she was alone.

At least here.

The white curtains rounded her on all sides. So privacy screens in a medical center. Well, that worked for her. Except she needed to know what was on the other side. She slowly sat up and kicked her legs over the side of the bed. Instantly the curtain was pulled back, and a woman dressed in medical whites, some kind of emblem on her shirt, walked over.

"Where am I?" Mia asked.

"You're in San Francisco at the Hartland Medical Center." The woman smiled down at her. "Now please lie back down and rest. Your body has been through a traumatic time and needs to heal."

Willingly, overjoyed with tears in her eyes, knowing she was safe, she snuggled back under the covers. The doctor covered her up.

"Are you still cold?"

Mia shook her head. "No, thank you."

"Good. How about other aches and pains."

"Yes," she admitted. "Everything hurts."

"To be expected." The doctor adjusted something hanging beside her and that was when Mia realized she was on an IV drip system.

"Am I badly hurt?"

"Nothing your system can't recover from. There are several broken bones in your face and a couple of cracked ribs. Your feet are damaged but in the soft tissue, so they only need time to heal. And the rest of you, well trauma can be a hard thing. The cold didn't help, but you're doing great considering what you've been through."

With another smile, the doctor left.

"Thank you," Mia called out.

"Don't thank me. I didn't jump into the cold water and haul you out," came the cheerful voice.

"Wait...what?" Water? Someone jumped in and hauled her out? Mia wracked her brain trying to figure out what water she was talking about. She remembered being a prisoner on a boat, but things were hazy after that. The one dominating theme was the freezing cold.

Vaguely she remembered sneaking up from below deck and hiding behind the rowboat. She didn't remember running into the water but must have. Or being pushed. No, she remembered feeling terrified of being caught. So she'd jumped.

Right...the memory jolted into her mind, but was distant as if from a dream. She'd grabbed a life preserver and jumped into the choppy waves. It had been so cold. She'd been kicking as hard as she could, but the waves had taken her where they wanted to.

And another memory blasted into her mind. Hawk. Or maybe a search and rescue person that reminded her of him. In her delusion, every man did. Sigh.

But she vaguely remembered being hauled up out of the water.

That was as far as her memory would go.

Warm and cozy, safe again for the first time in a long time, she closed her eyes.

Then opened them. Did they know about the bomb? Hawk. If they'd saved her, they must have found the fishing boat she'd been on. Except it ate at her. She had to know for sure. She sat back up and searched for a call button or cellphone, regular phone? Hell, a couple of Dixie cups and string would help. She smiled. No, they so wouldn't.

"Hello?"

No answer.

She frowned and pulled herself to the side of the bed. She did not want to hop down. She worried her feet wouldn't hold her. They shouldn't have been too badly damaged though. She'd been walking on the ship. She lifted a foot. It appeared fine.

As she checked the other one, suspicion rose. Maybe she wasn't so damn safe after all.

Slowly, she lowered herself to the floor and took a step forward. Her feet were puffy, hot. So the doctor was right. She glanced down at her clothing. Another hospital gown. White this time. Still, she had to know for sure. Nervous, she opened the curtain and peered outside. She was in a room with several other curtained off beds.

She was in a medical center. Thank God.

As she went to step toward the door, it opened. And several men entered.

She froze.

The man in the lead froze. And frowned.

"Damn it Mia, why aren't you in bed."

Hawk.

HE WANTED TO race forward and tie the damn woman down. He strode closer and glared at her. Gratified when she scrambled back into bed.

He deepened his glare for good measure and knew he'd failed to achieve his desired effect when she lifted her chin and glared right back.

"I'm fine."

"You're not fine. You're exhausted. Your body has been through a horrific trauma and you need to heal." Damn. How is it this woman always managed to make him yell? Even worse, her eyes now shone overly bright. She was crying. He felt like a heel.

Then she sniffled. That valiant warrior trying not to break down in the face of adversity. And he appeared to be the adversity this time. Damn it.

Her gaze widened as she looked behind him. The rest of the crew had crowded in close.

Her face brightened and she reached out her arms.

Hawk could only stare as big strong man Swede walked over and picked her up for a big gentle hug – after he shot Hawk a dark glare. Presumably for treating her so badly.

He rolled his eyes. Mia had Swede eating out of her hands. Shadow stepped up and took her from Swede and cuddled her close.

And she sank right in, loving the exchange. How the hell had she managed to tame each and every one of these huge bad ass men? His team were not teddy bears except with her...and Tesla, Mason's partner.

He didn't get it but watched in taciturn silence as each of his men hugged her gently. Even Dane who'd hardly met her got one. When Mason reached for her, she pulled back and stared at him for a long time, then smiled. "You're new, but I suspect you had just as much in saving me as the rest did, so thank you." And she gave him a big hug.

Mason turned with her still in his arms and stared at Hawk, a big grin on his face and a raised eyebrow.

Mia, comfortable in every one of this team's arms crossed her arms and announced to him with strong emphasis on the first word, "*Your* friends are very nice."

And she gave a short nod.

Like, what the hell.

It didn't help his team was grinning at him like the loons they were.

"No point in fighting it," Mason said. "Besides, I'm sure there are a few men here who want to know."

"What to know what?" he said in frustration.

Swede piped up. "Are you keeping her?"

CHAPTER 20

"**K**EEPING ME?" MIA cried. "No he's not keeping me. He doesn't even like me."

The others grinned. Shadow headed to the door, "Let us know, Hawk."

Hawk just shook his head, for once wordless.

Mason gently placed her back on the bed. "We'll give you two five minutes. Then we'll be back."

With a gentle smile, he dropped a kiss on her temple.

And walked out.

She watched them leave and had never felt so alone. "They're really nice. I don't want them to leave."

"They'll be back," Hawk said brusquely and sat down on the side of the bed.

"Why are they so nice to me and you're so mean?" she said in a forlorn voice.

"I'm not." But his tone was hard. Belligerent.

She shot him a disgusted look then pleated the sheets in a perfect line across her lap. Anything to keep her busy while dealing with him. He was so damn important to her, and everything she did seemed to be wrong. How did that work? "Why are you here?"

"This." He tugged her forward and into his lap.

And kissed her in the most gentle careful loving kiss she'd ever had. Tears came to her eyes. She wrapped her arms around his neck and lay in a fog of love as he caressed her puffy lips then kissed the damaged cheekbones, his lips as light as a butterfly's touch.

When he finally stopped and held her close against his heart, she whispered, "I must look at mess."

"You look as you always look," he said comfortably, "beautiful. Even more so now."

She snorted. "Wow, I didn't know you were injured too."

When he didn't respond, she leaned back and smiled. "Your eyesight must have gotten bad really fast."

He laughed. "Ha. Says you. You were always beautiful, now we know you're beautiful inside too."

And he kissed her again, this time harder, this time hotter. And it damn near melted her bones.

A cough behind them startled her. She tried to straighten, but Hawk wasn't having anything to do with it. He tightened his arms around her and said, "Go away."

Mason, humor in his voice, said, "Sorry Hawk, can't happen."

Hawk sighed. "Then come in and make yourself at home."

The others crowded around.

Mason gently said, "Sorry, Mia, but we need to ask you some questions."

She winced. "I understand." She struggled to put some distance between her and Hawk, settling back into place, tugging her covers up and over her. In an apologetic voice, she said, "It's my fault."

Hawk snorted.

She glared. Then her shoulders sagged, her irritation short lived as guilt took over. "I opened my mouth and I shouldn't have."

The men leaned forward as she recounted how she'd told the young officer, who she now knew wasn't an officer, about the knife and how she'd gotten it. And how she'd brought up the SEALs. "I didn't mention any names," she paused and frowned. "At least I don't think I did."

"Nothing you said mattered," Hawk said quietly. "The military was already involved."

"But you guys are super secret," she whispered. "And I think I said, 'Hawk told me someone was coming to pick up the knife.'"

They all nodded, but none seemed to think she'd made a major gaffe. She just *felt* like she had. With a deep breath and her fingers busy pleating the sheets, she finished off her story. Then fell silent.

Hawk reached over to cover her hands, bringing attention to the fact that she'd crushed a handful of sheet.

She trembled. "It really wasn't much fun," she muttered slowly, releasing the sheet.

"No, it wasn't, but it's over now."

She nodded. Then looked up at all of them. "Is it though? Did you find the fishing boat I was on?"

"We did, but it was in the process of sinking and it was empty."

"Crap. So they are still out there and still trying to do major damage?"

"We're on it," Mason said firmly. "That's our job. We've got this."

Hawk added, "And what's your job, Mia?"

She gave a half laugh. "To heal. And to stay where I'm put."

The others laughed. Hawk stood up. "I'll be back later and…" He glanced out the window then back at her. "Please stay safe."

And they were gone.

She leaned back, tears burning, but she refused to close her eyes. She really wished he'd kissed her good-bye.

Then he quickly returned and she was snatched, kissed hard enough to hurt but soft enough to not care, be-fore Hawk set her back down on the bed and said, "Stay safe."

She sighed happily. Her world was looking pretty damn rosy right now.

OUTSIDE HE STRODE down the hallway, his mind consumed with Mia. Damn it, she'd snuck into his heart and taken up residence. He hadn't expected it. The depth, the power of it all sidelined him.

The others were waiting for him at the end of the hallway. Grinning.

He glared at them.

Their grins widened.

It was only Mason who had a commiserating look on his face. He confirmed it when he said, "You might as well give in, you know."

"Give in to what," he snapped, knowing full well what Ma-son was talking about but not willing to acknowledge it.

"How you feel. It's over already."

"No, it's not," he said, more for form.

The others snickered.

"Take it from me," Mason said, "It's over."

Hawk slid a sideways glance at his friend. "Is it for you for sure?"

The smile on Mason's face made Hawk wish for the same thing. Did he have it? There was no doubt Mia was there in his heart. Could he ever imagine his life without her – hell no. But it had happened too fast. How could it be real? Could he trust it?

"That part is over," Mason said. "The rest is now just beginning."

Swede said, "You two lovebirds need to get your head in the game. And Hawk, was it wise to not tell her?"

Hawk shrugged. "I don't know. She has been through so much already. Besides, we told her we found the boat sinking."

"Yeah, but not that everyone on board had been shot dead."

"I didn't want to add to her worries."

"Yet she needs to know the players have changed," Shadow said quietly.

"She's out of it from now on," Hawk said, hating the doubt, the worry eating at him. Surely she was safe now. "She's safe here on base."

"We know for a fact that's not a sure thing," Swede said. "Look what happened to Tesla."

"No, but no one here is going to be involved in a terrorist plot like this," Mason said in a harsh voice. "I refuse to believe that."

"Just don't be blind to seeing the truth," Swede said. "Besides, they won't keep her here. She's going to be released to a hotel within hours. You know that."

"Then I need to make sure I'm at that same damn hotel,"

Hawk said. He looked over at Mason. "Let's just move her to a safe place now."

"She needs a guard."

He nodded. "Would be easier. Then we can run the shifts and keep an eye on her."

"We should have from the beginning."

"No, she needed treatment. Now she needs to stay safe. Hidden. That means secret her away somewhere safe."

"I'll do that," Cooper said as he joined them. He'd been waiting for them outside. Poor Cooper was still sidelined from active duty but he was a Godsend for handling the little details. "I'll send you the deets in an hour."

Leaving it in Cooper's hands, Hawk led the others back to the bay. To find the man who'd managed to kill everyone he'd hired so far.

He was now alone and on a mission.

Something they had to stop.

Fast.

CHAPTER 21

M IA FOUND HERSELF a fast two hours later ensconced in a hotel room somewhere in the city. She didn't even know where. Cooper, who she'd never met, but Hawk had vouched for, had made all the arrangements. Clothes had been provided including a flimsy nightgown. She hurt like a bitch but was in a wonderful bed, with painkillers taking the edge off everything else.

She just wanted to curl up and sleep. And she did, then woke up, used the bathroom and curled up to sleep yet again.

When the afternoon sun crept through the bright window, she was still drowsy but starting to feel human.

Almost.

She tried to get up, but the act of walking around the room to explore the area was more than she could handle, and she crawled back into bed.

This time she couldn't sleep.

And she was freakin' hungry. A knock sounded on her door.

She froze then shook herself out of her reverie, grabbed the matching housecoat to her nightie and walked over to peer through the tiny peephole.

Hawk.

Quickly she unlocked the door and let him in.

He looked exhausted but carried something that smelled wonderful.

She took the bag from him, afraid he'd drop it then nodded in the direction of the living room. "Go. You look like you're going to fall asleep."

He nodded. "I might but need a shower first." He started stripping his shirt off and dropping it, then his belt, followed by his shoes and pants. Each article dropped where they landed in the hallway and living room as he proceeded through the suite. By the time he'd hit the bathroom door, he wore only boxers. Then he disappeared from sight.

Crap.

She figured she couldn't be too badly hurt if she was more concerned about the sight of those heavily muscled cheeks being bared than the food in her hands.

But she could hear the water and realized he'd now be naked and…under that water.

If she knew what they had for a relationship, knew if she'd be welcome, she might have made her way into the shower with him. Considering the damage to her own body now and knowing how ugly and beaten up she looked, she figured he could have this shower alone. Maybe she could join him next time.

She put the food down on the table and quickly picked up his clothes, folded them and stacked them on the small chair, her mind busy on the image of water sluicing down his gorgeous body. Giving herself a mental shake, she forced her attention from one appetite to the other.

The food was Chinese. She grinned. Her favorite. Did he know? According to the conspiracy theory nuts, the military knew everything. Including her favorite foods.

Good. She was famished.

Her mouth was still sore, and she knew she'd be eating slowly and had to watch she didn't bite her lips. They were horribly swollen.

Likely would be for a few days.

She found two plates in the bag along with the napkins. She proceeded to ladle out the mix of dishes, her stomach moaning in joy at what was still to come. It looked wonderful. And he'd bought enough for the whole SEAL team.

Of course she might eat their share too.

She wanted to wait for him to join her, but she couldn't stop snacking. Finally she heard the door open and Hawk, dressed in a towel, walked out, refreshed but clearly exhausted.

But that damn towel marred a sculpture of beauty. She forced her gaze back to the plate in front of her. "Do you think you can eat, or do you need to go to bed…to sleep," she quickly corrected herself, "first."

He sat down in the chair beside her and let out a long careful breath. "We'll try food first." But his gaze never left her face.

Flustered, she picked up his plate and handed it to him. "Here. This is wonderful. Thank you so much for bringing it."

"Cooper ordered it and picked it up before he collected me."

She nodded. "He has great taste."

Hawk stared at the food on his plate then started to eat.

Like her, he appeared to be ready to wolf the entire plate down fast. And oddly enough, it was seeing how ravenous he was that helped her to slow down. She curled up with her knees under her and slowly ate, keeping an eye on him. "It was bad, was it?"

He paused and shoved the full fork into his mouth then

nodded. "It was."

That was all he said. She pondered that, realizing not only did no one know much about the SEALs, no one talked about them except in hushed whispers. Super secret spy stuff. She grinned at the phrase but understood that life with Hawk would often mean not talking about his work because he couldn't. And she had to be okay with that.

Considering the option was to not have Hawk in her life at all, she was *very* good with that.

Besides, he'd come home to her when he could. He'd talk to her when he could. And the rest of the time she'd trust him to do what he could to stay safe. That was all anyone could ask. Now, to get to the point of actually having a relationship. Trust her to lock down the fine print on a contract she didn't have yet.

He finally lay his empty plate down and leaned back with a happy sigh.

"Feel better?" she asked gently, now daintily picking at her food.

"Yes." He nodded to her plate. "Are you going to finish that?"

She laughed. "I am, but there is more in the containers."

He eyed the containers with interest, then shook his head. "Later. I'll have some later."

Later? What did that mean? After he got dressed? After a nap? Later tonight as in the middle of the night? She'd lost track of time, and had no idea what day it was.

"Did you let my father know that I was safe?"

"Yes, and Eva. No one else knows."

"No one else matters," she said. "Thank you."

"In truth, your father was contacting me every couple of

hours." Hawk grinned suddenly, boyishly. "I was grateful to be able to tell him something."

"We've only got each other now," she said quietly. "It would have destroyed him if I'd died."

"Not just him. You'd come to represent innocence to the world. The media is going to be all over you when you finally surface."

"Gross. I'm not anything to anybody. I'm just me." She hesitated then had to ask, "Did you find the men?"

He frowned, his gaze dropping.

"Shit. They are still out there, aren't they?"

"Someone is. But the men on the boat that held you captive, they were dead when we closed in on it. Someone was already cleaning up the details and had booked it."

What? She was shocked into silence. Then ventured, "And the bomb?"

"Gone, but there was enough threads and evidence left behind to figure out who is behind this," he said quietly. "But we haven't found him yet. We had an address but only found more bodies."

She stared. "The boss is really killing everyone off?"

He nodded. "We think so. Less men to tell tales this way."

"Do you still think he's planning to blow up the Golden Gate Bridge?"

"He's a terrorist so there's no way to know for sure, but the maps we found on the boat indicate they were actually after the Oakland Bay Bridge not the Golden Gate as we'd first thought."

"Oh good Lord." She slowly finished off her plate. "So all the work you've done on this so far was for naught."

"Not really. I think he was using the men and the fishing

boat as a trial run to figure out the kinds of problems he'd run into on his real expedition."

"Nasty."

"But typical."

"So now both bridges need to be guarded."

He grinned. "Absolutely."

She shook her head and placed her empty plate down on the coffee table then retook her seat. She hated the sudden awkwardness between them.

"Come here."

Her head flew up and she stared at him. He had his arms open. She narrowed her gaze and asked suspiciously, "Why?"

"Because you want to."

Damn his tone was smug. Then again he was right. She did want to.

She straightened and stood up, walked the two steps toward him and stopped. He motioned for her to sit down on his lap. She laughed. "Really. You want to cuddle. I figured you'd be ready for bed by now," she scolded.

"And maybe I am," he said, reaching up and tugging her onto his lap. "But it's good to hold you. Just cuddle and remember the reason why life is so precious."

Curled up in his arms, her hands laid against the warmth of his bare chest, she said, "You're right. I've done a lot of thinking about just that these last few days."

"Almost dying will do that to a person."

"Have you had that happen?"

He wrapped his arms around her and snugged her up tight. "Yes, I have. And had warm sunny days where I wondered what I was here for. Or why I was on this place called planet earth in the first place. And have often wondered, if there was more for me out there." He gave a half laugh. "Heavy philosophical thoughts for a military man, right?"

"Not at all. In your job you see a lot of the unpleasantness of life. And a lot more death than most people." She reached up to stroke the side of his face gently. "It's only natural that you'd think deeper than most."

"I suppose." He smiled down at her. "What made you so sweet?"

"I'm not sweet. Retiring. Shy. Insecure. Withdrawn even. Hard to step forward. Can't see myself in any kind of major role in life." Her nose got rapped for that. She laughed. "And I've often thought the exact same things as you. Wondering what my purpose in life is. If I had one."

"Of course you do." He dropped a kiss on her forehead. "We all do. It just might take a little longer to find it for some of us."

"Do you feel you have found it? Your place in the world?"

"Yes, but I also wondered what else there is, like I said. There's a part of me that feels something is missing."

"Missing?" She turned to look up at him, propping her arm on his chest. "Or...empty?"

"That was very intuitive of you." He leaned his head back and stared up at the ceiling. "But you're right. I've been alone, played lots, had many women, but lately..."

"It's not been the same."

"No. It hasn't been. And now I know why?" He tugged her up high against his chest and dropped a gentle kiss on her forehead. And another one on her nose. Then each cheek. She closed her eyes and relaxed against him as he kissed her closed eyelids, first one then the other.

Such peace as she'd never known descended on her. She snuggled her head into the crook of his neck and closed her eyes. How could such a strong man, so powerful in so many ways, strong yet controlled with that strength, be so tender?

She didn't know, but she loved it that he could.

And she was afraid that it would be hard to avoid falling in love with him.

If she hadn't done so already.

NOW THAT WAS much better.

She slept the sleep of an angel. Deep relaxed calm breaths, her body limp as it rested…and healed. She was a long way away from normal health, yet she was on the right path.

He knew he needed to stand up and move her over to the bed so she'd sleep properly, but it was so damn nice to just hold her.

His body wanted so much more. After a shitty day following several other shitty days, he wanted something to rejoice. She was safe and sound and that was huge, but having her be his, acknowledged verbally so there was no doubt in his mind she was his in all ways – now that was an ending he could wish for.

Sad to think he'd come to this.

Or maybe not. Like Mason, this was long overdue.

His angel shifted in his arms, trying to get comfortable. That had to be impossible. His protective instincts roused, he adjusted her in his arms, stood up and carried her to her bed. Thankfully the covers were still in disarray, so he could lay her on the sheets, managing to get the housecoat off, and cover her up. But there was no way he was going to leave her to sleep alone.

Not as tried as he was. He walked around and crawled under the covers on the far side. He'd lost his towel somewhere in the journey, and that was fine by him. He always slept in the nude.

She instinctively curled toward him. He tugged her closer. She snuggled right against him.

He smiled, and content for the first time in a long time, he slept.

CHAPTER 22

S HE WOKE TO a furnace. That was the only way she could describe this massive register of heat emanating off of Hawk. She lay still half asleep, her arm tucked up against his chest, his leg thrown across her legs pinning her in place.

The two of them entwined in the bed.

Nice.

His breathing was slow and deep. He'd been put through the ringer these last few days. She was sorry for her part in it but damn glad he'd rescued her. A girl could do a lot worse than snuggling up close to a hero.

She had to smile. She doubted he'd consider himself hero material. But he was all the way, right down to the heavy shadow on his face. Dark locks fell across his forehead that tempted her to reach up and straighten, but she didn't want to disturb him. Still Mother Nature called. She crept out of the bed and used the washroom.

When she snuck back in to the bed, he reached out and dragged her closer.

"Where were you?" he murmured in a sleepy voice.

"I had to go to the bathroom."

He opened his eyes. Took a moment to assess his surroundings, the timing, the moment, she could almost hear the answers clicking into place in his brain, before he came to a quick awareness.

Then he rolled above her, the weight on his elbows, settling himself exactly in the right place. And stared down at her.

She sucked in her breath as his erection prodded her sensitive skin. Oh Lord. She could feel her body wanting to weep in joy. She slid her hands up his chest, her gaze locked on his.

And waited. He searched her face as if looking for something. She wanted him to find whatever he needed but had no clue.

"Hawk?"

"Hmmm?" He lowered his head and dropped light tender kisses on her puffy face and she realized what he'd been looking for, healing. Signs that she was okay. That she was improving. That she was ready for this.

"I won't break, you know."

His mouth kicked up at the corner. "So you've proven several times already."

She laughed. "Well, I might have had a bone or two broken but...I'm feeling much better now."

"Shouldn't have happened in the first place."

"Maybe and maybe not. If it brought us here to this place...right now...I'm good with it."

She could feel his startled response and see the surprise lighting his dark gaze. Had she gone too far?

"I'd have done anything to have saved you from all of this," he whispered, his warm breath bathing her face as he kissed her cheekbone, his touch feather soft. Her other cheek received a kiss too.

A wave of emotion washed through her, and she reached up

and wrapped her arms around him and held him close.

"Love me," she wished. "At least for the moment. For a little while."

Scared to hear his response, she shifted so she could kiss him. She ignored her sore mouth and puffy lips. And kiss him she did. Trying to inveigle all the pain and longing she'd kept pent up inside her for so long. To let him know how he'd touched her. How he'd made her so much more than she was. That he'd been there for her when she'd been lost and that he didn't even know he'd saved her several times over.

When she went to pull back she realized he wasn't letting her go, he was kissing her back as long and emotionally deep as she'd kissed him.

Starting after a long lean lifetime, she sank into his embrace and let go.

For the first time ever, she let go in all ways.

She let him do what he wanted, how he wanted and then she did what she wanted. How she wanted. By the time he was ready to enter her body, she was shaking with emotion, trembling from the keen edge of pain and joy already racing through her body as he kept her on the cliff.

He entered slowly as if making sure to not hurt her. And he wouldn't. Ever. She wanted him. But not to hold back. She wanted all of him, now.

"Hawk," she cried out. "Now."

His dark laugh made her twist upwards, her body arching to receive all he had to give. She reached up and tried to tug him down to her. But he resisted. Instead he changed position and pulled her forward across his thighs then grabbed her hips to pull her tight up against his hips as he drove himself deeper.

She cried out as he touched her core.

"Am I hurting you?" he asked, his voice dark, guttural.

A laugh broke free. Clenching her tummy, she sat up tall and slid her arms around his neck, now under-standing why he'd been hesitating before. Her cracked ribs, collarbone. She smiled against his lips, "How do you feel about riding?"

He leaned back on his hands as she started to move.

"I love riding," he said in a fervent whisper. "Even better I love that you love riding."

Her laughter rang free as she held on to his shoulders and took them both to the edge – she paused – he groaned – and she moved faster.

He clutched her hips and pounded upwards.

And knocked her off the cliff. She cried out, arching back-wards.

He never lost his rhythm, his breath coming hard and fast, and giving one hard jerk, his seed poured inside her womb.

Tremors rippled over her skin as he gently lowered her to the bed, a fine mist giving both their bodies a warm glow.

She wanted to comment on it but didn't have the energy. Now she was damn tired. How did that work? She should be energized. And she was, but she was also just wanting to close her eyes and rest.

"Sleep. I'll find us coffee."

"Perfect," she whispered.

"No." He leaned over her as he snugged the sheet up to her chest. "You're perfect."

She fell asleep with a smile on her face.

"SO DAMN PERFECT," he muttered in a low voice as he stood a moment longer than he should. He forced himself to turn away and dress. Urgency was riding him. He was late. He knew it. He was never late. If he was today, the guys would know why. Shit. Then he stopped. Of course they'd know. And this time, he wanted them to know.

Yes, he was keeping her.

But they'd better not smirk at her. Or do anything that would make her uncomfortable. Then he sighed. They wouldn't. Not these guys. Not with anyone's lady friend. At least not a serious special one.

He was a lucky man.

And damn if he was going to be stupid about it.

He didn't know about that whole love thing, especially considering he'd never been in love before. But if wanting to whisk her away to a deserted island to keep her safe where she could have his babies and be his only for the rest of his life didn't qualify – he couldn't imagine what would.

His phone rang.

He checked the number. Cooper.

"I'm ready."

And with a last glance toward the bedroom, he walked out.

There was no way to know if he'd ever be able to walk back in.

In the car, he said to Cooper, "If you've got time..." he broke off.

"I've got it."

Hawk nodded. "Thanks."

"No thanks required. We all love her. You're a lucky man, Hawk."

He grinned. "Yeah I am and I know it."

Cooper pulled into the hanger just then. Hawk got out, ready to start his day.

CHAPTER 23

S HE WOKE UP with a smile on her face.
Until she realized the hotel room was empty.

Hawk was gone.

He'd said something about coffee. How long did that take? Order a little room service. Slip out to the coffee shop around the corner?

She had no idea. But there was a terrible finality to the emptiness.

Fear clutched at her heart. Had he meant to come back and couldn't? Had something happened to him? No, he was a SEAL. Of all the people who could take care of themselves it would be him.

She dampened down the fear. It was likely something simple – as in he'd been called away. That was all it would be. There was an imminent terrorist attack. Last night was stolen time.

She got up and showered, slowly running the soap over her body, reliving the night of loving. He was a masterful lover. Experienced. But more than that, he was so damn caring. Made her feel like the only woman in his life.

Of course he'd never said anything to her about tomorrows or even today, Neither had she after her initial plea – that she'd then not given him a chance to answer.

She'd figured he'd say the wrong thing to what she wanted to hear. And she couldn't have had that. She didn't want him to lie. Nor would she have wanted anything to change the magic of the moment.

She'd have missed something wonderful if she had. Now she couldn't stop remembering his hands as they'd slid over her skin, or the feel of his lips as he'd explored her ribs or the bones running up and down her spine. Was there any skin he hadn't touched? She rolled her neck, easing the stiffness. She'd slept so heavily her body ached in places she'd forgotten existed. Then again she probably couldn't blame her sleep for that. Hawk had been wild and creative and so damn strong.

She gave a happy sigh, shampooed her hair yet again and let the water flow over her head until it ran clear. Finally done, she stepped out of the shower and wrapped up in a towel.

The mirror caught her eye. A sparkling face shone back at her. A well loved face. Or rather, a well loved puffy face. She laughed.

Much of the swelling had gone down, leaving her face looking almost normal now. The lips were still puffy, but that could have been from Hawk's kisses.

Soon the evidence of what she'd gone through would be minimal.

And she could return to a normal life.

Whatever that meant.

She walked to her bed and sat down on the side. Did that matter? She was going home. Back to sharpen her search and rescue skills.

But that seemed so little now. Like an old life, not the life she wanted for herself. But she no longer knew what she wanted.

That was because she was no longer the same person. This had been a life changing event for her.

So what did she want?

She flopped back on the bed and considered that if all things were equal, what would she like to do?

She'd love to do more with her photography. Something she'd stopped doing because there'd seemed to be little point. Or maybe the truth was a lack of confidence. She'd done nothing with it, shown very few people the images she'd captured. But she could. Some were wonderful – at least to her. In her dreams, she'd love to produce coffee table books. Nice concept. But poor at paying the bills. Besides, she only took her camera on trips. She could hardly make trips to just take pictures – or could she?

Maybe she just wanted to do more. Helping Eva with the animals was nice and all, as they were awesome, but it was Eva's dream, not Mia's.

And the world had changed. Maybe picture books were possible, but they wouldn't be bestsellers.

She frowned. She didn't even know where her camera was. She'd been through so much shit she had no idea. She'd had it when she'd been caving. Then she got the message about her father being dead and everything after that had been a blank storm.

She no longer knew. Had it come back with their gear? And if it had, did it have anything she could use.

She got up and dressed in the clothes someone had taken the time to buy for her and made the bed. Hawk had promised coffee, but there wasn't any. Except her mind kept nudging her. Where had he gone? And was he coming back?

A knock on the door startled her. She froze then ran to the

door. Hawk?

She opened it without looking through the peephole. She knew instinctively she'd done the wrong thing.

Then she recognized the man in front of her.

Cooper. Hawk had mentioned something about Cooper not being on active duty as he was recovering from an accident. Apparently, he was happy to play nursemaid for her, holding coffee and a takeout bag advertising a local baker.

Her face fell. She stepped back and opened the door wider. "Hi Cooper." She mustered a smile for the man who'd been so good at organizing her life. "Right on time again."

"Actually, I'm running a little behind. Sorry."

He walked inside and handed her the coffee and the bag. "Breakfast for you."

She accepted both and leaned forward to kiss his cheek. "Thank you." Then she motioned to the couch. "Can you stay?"

He shook his head. "Not long."

She nodded and opened her bag. She gave him a fat grin as she saw the beignets. "Really? You found these here?"

He laughed. "Well, I certainly didn't fly these in from New Orleans."

She took the lid off her cup and sniffed the hot heady brew. "Lovely. Thank you so much."

She waved at him to sit down. "You're making me nervous standing up there. Is everything okay?"

He smiled, his face bland. "Of course."

She rolled her eyes. "Right super secret spy stuff."

With a big grin, he said, "Not quite."

The beignet was too enticing to resist. She took a big bite, sending a dusting of powder sugar everywhere. She chuckled.

Glancing over at him, she caught the worried look in his eyes. She slowly lowered the treat to the top of the package and laid it down. "What's the matter? Is he being sent out somewhere?"

Cooper shook his head.

"Right, he is, but you can't talk about it, and that's not why you're worried."

He raised both his eyebrows at that.

She slumped back. "I'm being sent home, aren't I?"

This time he did smile. "Don't think of it as being sent home. Consider it more a heading home to safety time."

"And yet that's where I was kidnapped from."

He nodded. "We know. You're welcome to stay here of course. There's no one forcing you, but in our opinion, you should be at home with your father."

She nodded. "It is time, I guess."

She'd been thinking about that just a little while ago but hoping against hope that there'd be Hawk running through the door asking her to stay with him forever. She was a fool. He was never going to say that.

"I do have a problem."

He frowned. "What's that?"

"I don't have a way to get home." She glanced down at the clothes she was wearing. "And did you provide these? If so, thanks."

He nodded. "They look good on you. And thank Hawk, he gave me the size and told me what to get."

Of course he did. Somehow his years of experience with women had given him a trained eye to know exactly what size she wore.

Figured.

There was no reason to stay now. If Cooper said it was time to go home then Hawk wasn't coming back.

So she'd be staying for nothing.

And in that case, she'd rather go home. "I could leave any-time if I had a way to get home."

"I was hoping you'd say that."

She raised her eyebrows and looked at him over the cup.

"Your father is on his way," he said. "To pick you up."

HE COULD SENSE the other men watching him. Wanting to say something but not actually giving voice to the words. Too bad. It would ease the tension around them. What did they expect him to do? She needed to go home. At least until this nightmare was over.

If he survived this mission then he might look her up. Re-gardless of his thoughts early this morning about keeping her, he wasn't a good bet. There was always another mission. This was a tough job. He couldn't tell her much about it, and he'd always be on the road.

But damn it was an impossible thought to let go of.

Besides, they were approaching the ship they were prepared to board. Hardly the time. As the Coast Guard vessel they were riding in came along side, he pulled his mask down and slipped overboard. They were looking for the bombs. The intel had been solid. But so far, finding the goods, that was a whole different story.

And this could go easy or it could be a shit storm. He swam around down below the front of the tanker to the small fishing boat tied up on the far side. It was the twin to the one they'd rescued Mia from. While the Coast Guard took care of the crew, his team would check out the fishing crew. If there were any.

He signaled to Swede and swam up. He rose slowly, checking out the size and breadth of the vessel. It was big enough and had a small lift on the back so it could have easily lifted the bomb off. Once in the water, it would be easy to drag the device into position.

They worked to the back of the fishing boat and slipped aboard. It was empty. They gave it a quick search. There were bits and pieces of wires left behind and some powder on the floor. A worktable. Ropes.

He messaged the Coast Guard about what he found.

After another quick search, they retraced their steps and slipped back into the water. And went straight down toward the bridge pylons. They were down long enough the air became an issue. They gridded the space and searched the entire area. And found nothing. Back at the Coast Guard they switched tanks and a second team joined them in the search. The Coast Guard motored over to the next rendezvous. Six hours later they'd checked out all the points they'd had marked. And still nothing.

Afterwards, pissed and exhausted, they met to reevaluate.

"We can't have missed it."

"No. Therefore it's not there."

They stared at each other in frustration. "If not there, where?"

Mason's phone rang. His conversation was short, explicit. When he put away the phone he said, "We've found one."

That set up a series of conversations and another plan.

This time the trip would end differently.

CHAPTER 24

L IFE AT HOME had a different edge to it.

Mia loved having her father back. The attack and loss of his brother had him taking an interest in the store again. He'd been reorganizing it after the vandals finished. Oddly enough there was mostly candy and gum missing. She had a good idea who to blame for that, but as she hadn't seen Tom's son and his cousin since her return, she couldn't be sure. After all, his father had been involved in her kidnapping. That he'd gotten his comeuppance was one thing, but to imagine that his son was part of this was a different thing altogether. There was an uncle around somewhere as well, but she had no idea where. And she didn't want to know.

Things had been quiet.

For that she was thankful.

"Mia, can you bring the horses over here. The farrier will be arriving soon," Eva called out.

Mia chucked at the two retired quarter horses Eva fostered. Amongst other animals. Then Eva had a heart as big as the acreage she owned and lucky for the animals, did something with it – for both.

She walked toward Eva, knowing the horses would follow on their own accord. They were big babies and loved to be with their people friends.

She opened the gate and stepped back so they could move toward Eva. All animals loved her. Always had. If the truth be told, Mia was slightly jealous.

She wished she had something to do. Something special she *could* do. She really wanted to do search and rescue on a bigger scale. Only that would mean leaving Canford. And she wasn't ready to do that.

She watched her friend as she spoke to the horses and the llama that was on the other side of the fence. She had a good dozen animals here she fostered. And so many more she'd adopted. She was alone and appeared to love it that way. Eva said she hadn't met anyone that made her want to change her status.

Mia had said the same thing until she'd met Hawk. Only he was a distant memory now. But one that made her smile. She didn't begrudge his presence in her life, only that it was now in her past.

Her father walked over. "Mia, you okay?"

She smiled up at him. "Sorry, just daydreaming."

He closed the gate behind her and wrapped an arm around her shoulder. "Are you sure you're okay?"

"I'm fine. Healing well."

"Are you?" He studied her face as if looking to see if her bones actually healed under the skin. "The ribs?"

"Better." She walked ahead of him. "I'm back to normal."

"That's not true."

She turned to look at him. "In what way?"

"You're sad all the time."

Her head shake was instinctive. "I'm not," she protested. Yet she was lying. She knew it, but as nothing could change the situation she was determined to move forward.

"You are. At first I thought it was because of what you've gone through. Maybe it is?"

"Maybe," she said noncommittally, wishing she could get out of the conversation before her father guessed the real reason.

"As long as you're mending." And he walked toward Eva, his own gait unsteady and stilted. He used a cane now, but that beat wheelchairs out any day. "Interesting thing about an event like that," he said. "It changes us forever."

"Or maybe for just a little while," she said with forced cheerfulness.

"I hope so. You've been through enough. You deserve to be happy."

Did she though? She hated that she felt guilty for mentioning Hawk's name to the young cop in the hospital. A terrible blunder. And one she'd paid for. But it had given her a scare. She'd survived, but what about other victims of crimes? Did she want to do something more to help? The questions roiled through her head in an unceasing hamster wheel.

After they were done helping Eva, her father dropped her off at her trailer.

"I wish you'd move back home again," he said.

"Not going to happen Dad." She laughed and waved good-bye to him.

He shook his head and drove off, calling out, "Come for dinner tomorrow night."

"Okay, will do," she yelled back, waving good-bye.

With a smile, she headed back into her trailer. She could have walked the short distance from the barn but her dad was more concerned about making sure she got home safe and sound.

Not that anything more was going to happen to her.

This was her house. With a big smile at the wide world around her. The birds sang, the tree branches swayed in the wind as the fresh air blew down the valley. It was a beautiful day.

Inside she put the teakettle on. While it was heating, she took off her jacket and boots. The phone rang. She answered to find Paul checking up on her.

"I hear you're home safe and sound."

"Yep, I'm back."

"Good, ready to go caving again?"

"I'm not sure I'm ready for that yet." But she should be. It was part of her promise to herself to get back to living. She could do a caving trip. After all she'd been through, it was going to be easy. "I'm not sure I'm physically strong enough."

"We could just do a gentle trip. Go into the first couple of caves. Try a different system."

"It would have to be a short one," she warned. "I'm not back to full strength."

"Right. That's no problem." He laughed. "We can always carry you out if need be."

"Not going to happen." But she chuckled at the thought.

"Good, so tomorrow then? Say eight am?"

"Damn, make it a little later. I'm not up so bright and early these days."

"Okay, nine it is, but no later. We don't want to be returning too late in the day."

"Just a short excursion though, right?"

"Absolutely."

At that she rang off with a smile on her face. She had good friends. With his call, she felt like she'd really come home.

"NOW WHAT?"

The men looked at each other.

"Rest and recuperation time," Swede said. "We got the bombs, got the men and missed the boss."

"Not for long. We'll get him," Shadow said in that slow drawl of his. "But we need new intel."

And that was the problem. They'd lost track of the boss and any of his henchmen, if there were any left. The head of the terrorist cell had gone underground but had left a mess of dead bodies in his wake. Cleaning up.

Frustration ate into Hawk's gut. He wanted the boss captured – or better yet – dead. There'd been no leads in the last four days. He'd likely left the country. They needed to know where. So far everything had come up empty. Until then there was no time off. And Hawk couldn't determine if that was good or bad.

"The orders just came through," Mason said. "We're to take a few days off. Get back in time to move on the intel they're gathering in the meantime."

Hawk stared at Mason. "Really?"

Mason nodded. "I'm going to spend my days by Tesla's side." He paused. "Are you?"

"I hadn't asked Tesla if she was ready for company," Hawk said, deliberately misunderstanding.

"And Mia, is she?"

"No idea." He stood up. "Not my problem."

Mason nodded. "In that case, I can ask Swede."

Hawk froze. He slowly raised his head to look at Mason,

catching the smirk on his face. "Why would you ask Swede?"

"Because as I understand it, the guys plan on visiting both Mia and Eva. At least Swede and Dane are."

"And the women know they are on the way?"

He shrugged. "I doubt it."

He loved the guys, but he didn't trust them around women. They'd never poach but they'd certainly rile things up.

He turned back to the door. "So are you coming to visit Tesla and me or are you…" Mason stopped and raised an eyebrow at Hawk.

"Damn." Hawk shot him a disgusted look. "You know exactly what I'm going to do." He reached into his pocket and pulled out his keys.

"Say hi to Mia. I'll bring Tesla up to visit one of these days," Mason said laughingly.

Hawk's jacket was on the back of the chair. He snagged it up, threw it over his shoulder and walked to the doorway.

CHAPTER 25

THE CAVE ENTRANCE was lit in sunshine. She was happy to see it. She'd woken in a great mood and was looking forward to being out and about today. She needed to know that her body was working the way it was supposed to.

She knew she wouldn't be able to pass a physical right now. Running was out of the question. And that was definitely something she needed to get back doing again. Except she was still so exhausted.

But she was here and that was good.

A little bit every day. She'd have her strength back in no time. And she didn't want to be so weak any more. She'd been through too much to want to be back into that helpless mode again. So self-defense training was next. "It's a beautiful day."

"It is, that means it's a lovely day to go caving," Paul said, coming to stand beside her.

"How did you think that? It's beautiful to be topside so that means we should go into the dark?" She laughed at his logic.

"Think about the joy of seeing the world underground in all that shadowy beauty then coming to the surface to see the glorious sun." Peter and Paul grinned in unison at her. "It's a special world down there."

"You two are special nuts," she said with a laugh. "Lead on."

"I'm in front, then you," Paul said. "My brother will bring up the rear."

"All right. You just want to make sure I don't screw up."

"No, we want to make sure you're up for this. If you collapse we can get to you faster this way."

"And I appreciate it." She did too. These two men had been keeping an eye on her since she'd started her search and rescue work. She trusted them. When going into caves it was important to trust the people you were with.

The two men were retired and spent the bulk of their time exploring the natural caves around them. And shared their love of their hobby with anyone who'd listen.

She strapped on her hard hat, adjusted it in place, checked her riggings then fell into place between the two.

"Let's do this."

The walk at the beginning was light and breezy. It felt good to move her body the way it was supposed to move. To feel her muscles groan when they stretched. It would take an hour to really loosen, but this activity felt good. Her ribs ached slightly and her face was still tender if poked too hard. But the doctors here had been pleased with her progress.

Now she just needed to deal with the rest of the shit in her life. Maybe more rescue volunteering. After all, who knew better than her about being in need of saving? Still, that was only part of the answer.

"Brought your camera again, did you?" Peter asked. "Gonna turn us into cover models."

She grinned and after adjusting the lighting quickly snapped a photo of him. "There, now I can submit you to those romance stock photo sights." And she laughed.

"Ha, girlie, I could show them a thing or two."

She grinned. "Gray and grizzled is a popular look. There's at least a third of the population looking just the same."

The two men snorted in mocking disgust, but it set the tone for the next few hours as they took a different pathway through the caves.

"Did you guys map all this section yet?"

"We're just about done. There's at least one more to check out. After that we should be able to map it down and call this system quits."

"Anything glorious here?" she asked. "An underground river? A fantastic waterfall?"

"No. Lots of ways in and out. Another entrance someone else appeared to have found as there are truck tracks driving right into it. Had no idea one of the entrances was big enough."

"It likely wasn't," Paul said. "Probably they widened it to get that truck in."

Mia stilled at the sound of a truck in one of the cave entrances. That brought back images and memories she wasn't ready to revisit.

"Is that close by?" she asked in a neutral tone. She had no idea if Hawk's team had managed to put a stop to the bombing or not. There'd been no coverage in the news about it so she presumed so, but that wasn't the same as knowing for sure. It was as if the whole thing never happened. She might be okay with that, but a little closure would help.

"It's not far. Why, do you want to swing by and take a look? That entrance would be a huge boon in case of an accident. Big enough to bring an ambulance in. Not sure it's big enough for a search and rescue truck, but it might be."

"It would be good to know either way," she said. "How many people have been out here this morning al-ready?"

"A half dozen at least. It's getting more popular every day. We're really hoping to find something major to bring in more people," Paul said.

"That would create a lot of business to the small town," she admitted.

"What about you? What are you going to do now that you're back? Is your father opening the store again?"

She frowned, still uncomfortable with the concept of being back and having a future. "I think he's going to reopen but on a smaller scale."

"No guns." The two brothers nodded sagely. "I imagine he's done selling those," Peter said.

Paul added, "Not done owning them though."

"No, Dad isn't ever going to get rid of his personal collection."

"I did see him at the shop cleaning up. Maybe in an end re-sult this has been good for him. He can heal now and get back on his own two feet."

"Maybe," she said. "Or maybe he's going to sell up and move to downtown LA."

At the men's horrified looks she chuckled.

"In that kind of mood, are you? Well, let's add a side trip here so you can see the new entrance. Maybe an extra hour of work will take some of that punch out of you."

He led the way to the left. She followed, her early joviality wearing thin by the time they arrived. Her energy was flagging quickly. Damn. As a check to doing rescue work again, she'd seriously failed. There was no point in going out to help people if she was going to need rescuing herself. She'd known that but had hoped to find herself in better condition than this.

"It's not much further," Peter in front of her called out.

"Good. I'm getting tired," she admitted.

"We'll rest here," Peter said behind her. "And if it's that bad, I'll go back, grab my truck and pick you up. That's another big advantage of this new entrance. We were quite excited when we saw it," he added in a con-versational tone. "We don't want the caves to be too easy, but there's no doubt that easy is a help at times."

They approached a small short tunnel that was more of a cave in that it left a bit of room to navigate through. Still she could tell it was an old cave by the undisturbed dusting on the ground. It was trickier going but short. It suddenly opened up into a big opening that she swore was bigger then the entrance they'd come in through originally. Interesting.

It always amazed her how there could be such big pockets of nothing in these mountains. It always seemed safe inside but she had to wonder.

A yawn caught her by surprise.

Paul motioned to the far side where there appeared to be just ore wall. She walked closer and realized the cave curved slightly and the entrance was full of greenery blocking the sunlight from entering.

She peered out then carefully picked her way through to stand under the bright light. "You said a truck came through here?"

"Yeah, these branches," he pointed to the stripped side of the some larger branches, "were damaged in the process."

"Amazing." She picked her way through the dense underbrush following the tracks and came to a small clearing. "It's hardly a road."

"And that's good. Roads mean traffic. We really don't want people to have too much access."

"Right."

The three of them wandered in the sunlight looking for where the access to the main roads were, following the truck tracks a little way.

"There it is." Paul pointed down at the hill below them. "It's just off Hairpin Bend."

She studied the nasty corner and realized he was right. And that wasn't a bad location. The main road was a few hundred meters off which meant she could have help to this corner of the caving system at least a half hour faster than the other entrance. Realizing people could be stuck anywhere in between meant this new entrance could save lives.

"This is a fantastic find," she said.

"Yeah, figured."

She pulled off her hat and turned her face to the sunlight.

"You're looking a little piqued," Paul said, worry in his voice.

"I'm okay. A little tired but seeing this," she waved at the easily accessible entrance, "has given me more energy."

"Still, we're going to go back, grab both vehicles and come here. See how hard it is to find the entrance from the other side. That's the trick. It's one thing to be on the inside wondering where everyone is but another if you're driving the truck, which I often am, trying to find the new entrance."

She sat down on a fallen log and realized he was right. She was too tired. One brother could go or both. It would be faster if both left to pick up their truck and car. Save a return trip to pick up the other set of wheels. "Okay, so you're heading back inside and I'm napping here." She smiled up at the two men. "Sounds good to me." It really did. She unbuckled her rope harness and stretched out on the log. "See you in what, thirty minutes?"

"We're that long just getting back to the main entrance if not half that again so make it an hour."

Peter hesitated. "You okay to be here all alone?"

"I'm fine." She waved them off. "Go."

"Okay back soon. And keep your phone on you. We'll text you as we get to the vehicles."

She nodded but was already closing her eyes, her body sore and weak. Damn. Who knew a couple of hours of cave exploration could wipe her out so quickly. She'd be weeks getting her strength back at this rate.

So not helpful.

With the heat of the sun beating down on her, she was forced to open her jacket and keep her water close by. She closed her eyes and took a deep sigh of contentment, letting her body relax into the tree beneath her back.

Until a hard voice spoke from behind her.

"So there you are. You've led me a merry chase, haven't you?"

HAWK DIDN'T KNOW if Mason had been kidding when he said the other men were on their way to see Eva and Mia, but he wouldn't put it past them. Dane had been particularly interested. Too damn bad for him. He wasn't going to give Mia any warning. He didn't want to give her a chance to say no. He wouldn't handle that well.

They hadn't said anything between them. And he'd left without an explanation of his impending departure, nor had he contacted her since they got back, but that didn't mean there wasn't something between them.

There'd always had been something there.

But she'd been through a major trauma and needed to heal. And he didn't want her to see him only as a hero. Nor as a SEAL. He was just a man.

Eva would keep an eye out for her, but that wasn't the same thing as Mia being aware enough to look after herself the way she should. She'd need several more weeks to heal. Not volunteering for anything and everything.

By the time he'd driven for an hour, he'd worked himself into frustration. He figured she was probably overdoing everything again. And wouldn't stop unless someone was there to curtail her activities.

She never did have any sense.

But she had raw guts in spades.

Now he had to get there before his damn men. If they got in ahead of him, they'd never let him live it down. And neither would she. Especially, if she didn't realize he was on the way.

He slammed his foot down on the gas pedal and ripped past the slower traffic. He should be there in just over an hour.

Hopefully in time to stop her from getting in trouble again.

CHAPTER 26

HER NERVES SHOT off the scale, her heart pounded against her ribs and her body was suddenly wearing a film of fear. Dear God. When was this shit going to be over?

"Sit up."

She slowly sat up, her water bottle in her hand, and turned to face the stranger. She studied his features. "I don't even know you."

"No, you don't. I prefer it that way. I'm a professional and part of that is cleaning up loose ends."

"What do you want from me?"

"Nothing now. Except to extract a little vengeance. They found my bombs. I couldn't do what I promised to do because of you, so now I'll be executed for failing."

"They?" she asked cautiously.

"It doesn't matter who *they* are," he snapped. "In fact nothing matters anymore. You put a stop to my mission. In the eyes of the world, I'm a failure."

"I had nothing to do with it," she cried. "I don't know what mission you're talking about."

"Don't be stupid." He snarled. "Your friends might have stopped me from destroying the bridge, but they can't stop what I'm going to do next."

She shook her head. "I don't understand what any of this has to do with me."

"If you hadn't been involved then the damn SEALs wouldn't have been involved."

He knew about Hawk? How could that be? She stared at the man who made no sense, but the fanatical look in his eyes said he thought he did. "I had nothing to do with the SEALs stopping you. I was kidnapped, then escaped." She shook her head. How damn stupid. At least the two Bangor brothers were gone. They'd be spared bullets this time around. She'd likely end up wearing all of them.

"Your men were the weak link," she snapped with more force than she planned. "I just dove into the water and was picked up by the military helicopter."

"And told them everything."

She stared at him. "Well of course I did. But it's not my fault the men you hired were shit."

He waved his gun at her. "It doesn't matter. I knew you were trouble right from the beginning."

"Then why didn't you shoot me?"

"The idiot Tom wanted to find out what you'd learned and said about him. He was afraid you'd blown his game here."

"And instead you blew a hole in him."

"Sure I did and all the other men I worked with. That's the way I work. I hire then terminate." He shrugged as if to say that was completely normal behavior for a boss. "It's really the only way. You can't trust anyone you know."

She stared at him. "That's not true. You can trust a lot of people in this world."

He snickered. "Then you're a fool. But a dead one."

He lifted the gun and fired.

She'd already moved. Bolting in a zigzag motion, she made the safety of the cave. There she had one ad-vantage. She knew the area – somewhat.

"You can't hide in here," he yelled at her.

She wanted to yell back at him but couldn't let him know where she was. Hiding around the corner, she considered her options. Try to sneak outside again when he came inside or try to return through the cave system to the other entrance.

"See, I can sit here and wait all day. Especially for your friends to come back."

She could feel her face bleaching in shock. The brothers wouldn't know what they were walking into. He'd shoot them instantly. They hadn't done anything. Neither had she, but apparently she was the one loose thread he'd take pleasure in putting down.

Great.

A scrape sounded too damn close. She flattened against the wall. Depending on the angle, he wouldn't be able to see her unless he came further in. She gripped the hard hat in her hand. As a weapon it wasn't much.

"There's no point in hiding. You're just going to prolong the agony," he called out. "I can wait all day for you."

She closed her eyes and opened her mouth, her breathing shallow, thin.

Now what was she going to do? She tried to estimate the time since the brothers had left. She'd napped for a while there. But not likely more than ten minutes, maybe twenty at the most. If there was any help coming it wouldn't be for a half an hour and that was a huge time frame to stay alive. She'd have to escape on her own again.

She'd rather be lost in the caves and need rescue than take a bullet to the head. This man was going to make sure she was dead.

His footsteps receded as he walked back to the entrance way. "That's okay. I'll wait for your friends to show up and kill them first. Then come after you."

She closed her eyes. She didn't want the brothers to die. She pulled out her cell phone and shut off the sound. She checked for a signal. None.

Of course she'd need to be closer to the entrance to get a message out. She peered around the corner to see him standing and staring out at the world, his back to her. Too bad she didn't have a gun herself right now, she'd take him out where he stood. Her mind raced, she tried to think. If she ran back to the original entrance, the brothers would likely be here by then, alone and vulnerable to attack. If she stayed here, they'd arrive with no warning and be killed anyway. She needed to get a message out. Were any of the other caves in this system closer to the outside world? No. That was why they were here.

She leaned her head back, angry tears forming at the corner of her eyes. She had to find a way.

She'd warned her father and Eva that she was heading down to the caves with the brothers so if she was late they'd know where to find her. But she wasn't late yet. In fact, she wouldn't be late for a while. And being with Peter and Paul, no one would worry for quite a while. She might have to try and sneak out.

What other choice was there?

Hawk drove into the town limits and called his sister.

"Hawk? Where are you?"

"I'm just entering town," he snapped. "Why?"

There was an odd pause and she said gently, "Because we didn't think you'd be coming back any time soon."

He didn't have to ask who the "we" was. "Where is she?"

"She went caving this morning."

"She what?" he roared. "She's sick. Needs to heal, not crawl in the dirt." Damn that woman. He'd been driving like a crazy man for hours trying to beat his friends. He hadn't seen them yet, but ever since he'd started out at a hell bent pace he couldn't seem to stop the worry that she wouldn't be there when he arrived.

"She wanted to see if she was back to normal strength," his sister said calmly. "It's not like it was easy on her to come home. She kept seeing boogeymen everywhere. She's trying to deal."

"I know." He didn't offer an apology. Acknowledgement was the closest he was going to get. "I didn't mean to snap." He glanced at the signs coming up. "Any idea which caving system she's at?"

It was a dim thought in the back of his mind that maybe he could catch her at the caves. Give her a ride home. After he tore a strip off her for being out there in the first place.

"The brothers are mapping Grossman Caves. So she'll be there somewhere." His sister added in a careful voice, "I don't think she's expecting to see you."

He snorted. "Of course not."

And he hung up. His instinct was correct. The signs up ahead were for the caves. Tires squealing, he made the sharp turn and raced up the dirt track. From the look of the road it was a popular place. She better have gone with a decent group. If she got too tired, someone needed to be capable of looking after *her*.

Grinding his teeth, he plowed the Jeep over the rough roads.

CHAPTER 27

"I CAN WAIT all day, I don't have any plans," the gunman said. "Only I won't have to because pretty damn fast, you're going to have company."

She closed her eyes, sweat running down her back. This was so damn stupid. She'd done nothing and here she was in trouble again.

Hawk would have her hide if he knew. Hopefully he'd never find out.

She could hear distant sounds of an approaching vehicle and frowned. It was revving too high for the brothers. Shit, please let it not be another group of innocent tourists. She didn't want to be responsible for more deaths.

"Do you hear what I hear?" He laughed, but it was a harsh sound of impatience. As if he wasn't happy about company coming either. "Get out here now or more people are going to die."

The back of the cavern beckoned. By her count, it couldn't be the brothers as they wouldn't have had time to get this far yet. But her options still hadn't changed. She could run and hide in the cave and hope he left with time – without killing anyone, or she could go out there and take a bullet. Like that was happening.

The vehicle approached. She heard a sound she recognized. Her heart leapt in hope. Was that a Jeep? She'd been around trucks and Jeeps all her life. Hawk drove one, but there was no reason to consider this was *his* Jeep.

Was the asshole still there? She snuck back and peered around the corner of the cave. The killer had retreated to the cave in front of her, his back to her again. It pissed her off to have him consider her so small a threat. Glancing around the rough ground, she searched for rocks to use as a distraction – or weapon. But considering how lousy a baseball player she'd been, she figured she might be better able to warn the newcomers away before he could get a shot off. Then she'd bolt back into the cavern and track her way back to the other entrance. Chances were good she'd be able to outrun him in here. She knew where to go.

The vehicle roared up to the front of the cave and came to a halt just on the other side of the bushes. She couldn't see the driver. Apparently the killer could. He lined up his handgun to take a shot.

She swung her arm and fired off the first rock.

Hitting his hand.

The gun fired.

Birds flew from the trees and both she and the killer froze in shock.

He unfroze first and the gun spun and lined up with her in its sights.

She gasped, tucked back out of sight and grabbed more rocks. The edge of the wall she was hiding behind was rough with a staggered edge. As quietly as she could, she climbed upward, her pockets full of rocks. If he came around the corner, he'd be looking for someone shorter than him, and she might manage to get a couple of good kicks in.

The Jeep hadn't fired up again. She hoped the shot hadn't found a target after all.

Something scraped the wall just feet for from where she crouched.

"Bitch," he said in a low lethal voice. "Think that was funny, do you?"

The gun slipped around the corner first, followed by his head as he tried to look on the other side of the corner. Her first kick slammed into his jaw, the second sent the gun flying.

She landed on her back but was up and racing to the entrance as fast as she could. And another shot rang out. She stumbled as something tugged at her sleeve, but she kept on running. The Jeep was up ahead. Please let the keys be in the ignition, please!

Not ten feet from the driver's side door she was tackled from behind.

"No," she screamed and fought with all she had, sending her elbow into her attacker's throat and her knees to his groin as she reached forward to find something to bite on.

"Damn it," Hawk snarled and she suddenly found herself crushed against his chest and dragged behind a big rock. "Stop struggling."

In truth she hadn't been struggling since realizing who held her. "He's trying to kill me," she whispered. "He blames you guys for stopping his terrorist mission."

Hawk spun, stared at her as if asking for confirmation.

She nodded at him. "It's the terrorist who organized the bombing."

HE COULDN'T BELIEVE it. Why hadn't he considered that after foiling his plans the guy might go after loose threads? Hell, he'd killed everyone else he'd hired, so why not go back after their captive who'd gotten away. That must have really chafed at him.

Now he'd found Mia here alone. Vulnerable. Easy. A perfect target.

He glared at her for good measure. She raised her eyebrows in confusion.

Yeah, he'd clarify as soon as he got her out of this trouble and taken out the guy they'd hunted over several continents. Only to find he'd returned to where it had all started.

Shit.

And he didn't have his gun with him. First thing was first, keep Mia safe. He pushed her deeper into the shadows. He'd give her the Jeep and send her away to safety, but he had no doors on it for summer, making her a big target.

The shooter was pinned down at the entrance to the cave but might know enough to disappear into the correct passages.

He could hope. But if he'd been part of a gun caches here, he could be an expert on this cave system.

With Mia carefully tucked behind him, he slid down the brush toward the opening. He needed to get this guy. As long as he was loose, he was a danger. He'd already proven what lengths he'd go to clean up his trail. Now that Mia had seen him, she was doubly at risk. They had to bring this to an end before the terrorist went underground, free to choose his time and place later. This had to end now.

He quickly sent a text to Swede and Shadow. Dane was next.

If they were in Canford, he could use them now. He studied the layout. Given where he and Mia stood, neither could move without giving away their locations and as only one of them had brought a gun to the gunfight…

A surprise noise behind him made him spin around. Mia had armed herself with a decent sized branch. She swung it several times, getting used to the feel of the weight in her hand. She caught his glance and whispered, "I do feel better with a weapon."

Hell, so did he.

"I don't know who the hell is out there, but you're not going anywhere," yelled the killer.

Hawk laughed. "Neither are you."

An ugly silence fell.

"Who the fuck are you?"

"The man that stopped your operation," Hawk said, already moving and shoving Mia ahead of him as bullets fired randomly, wildly into the bush where they'd been standing. He grinned, a hard edged anger of his own coursing through him.

Another vehicle could be heard in the distance. Good, hopefully that was his team.

Only Mia gasped and clutched at him. "It's likely the brothers."

It took a moment to understand. He placed his mouth against her ear and said "Is there another entrance close by where we can go in and come up behind him?"

She nodded. "But it's not a short hike."

"How long?"

"If done hard and fast, one hour and forty-five minutes," she said in a low voice, looking around. "If you run and grab the brothers coming down, you can ride to the next entrance and do it in forty-five."

He gave her a hard kiss. "Stay here. Climb a tree and get the hell up and out of sight. I'll be back in thirty minutes."

She gasped but he was already gone.

CHAPTER 28

S URELY HE WAS joking. But he'd disappeared so fast she could only see the cloud of dust he'd kicked up. And that meant she was alone again. She ran her hand over her head, wondering where the hell she should go without making a sound.

Had the killer heard Hawk leave? The second vehicle was no longer approaching. She hoped that had been the brothers. They'd help out and consider it an honor to do so.

But she wished they'd picked her up too. Hawk could move faster without her. But it didn't make her happy to be stashed behind a rock. Although he'd said to climb a tree, she couldn't do so quietly. A huge evergreen with low lying boughs grew ten feet away. She might be able to sneak into the middle of that tree. It would offer better protection than her current spot if the killer decided to come out looking for her.

For them. As he had no idea Hawk had left. And that was her saving grace. Alone she didn't pose much threat. But with Hawk here, then the killer's odds just went down. Even with a gun. Still he'd be focused on taking Hawk out after hearing who he was.

Hating the feeling of being a sitting duck, she scooted over and slid under the heavy foliage. With fear making her hands shake, she backed up until she was against the trunk. If nothing else, she could bolt in the other direction and dodge her way through the trees. He'd have a hell of a time hitting her then.

Closing her eyes, she mentally called out to Hawk to hurry his ass.

And he'd better take care of it too – she had visiting rights, damn it.

At least, she hoped she did.

"Where the hell are you?" Bullets fired to the left of her, but his voice, it was getting closer. She curled up into a tiny ball and buried her face in her arms. Her clothes were already dirty from the caving…shit, shit *shit*. She had her reflective straps on her vest. He'd see her for sure.

Heart slamming heavily, her gut was ready to upchuck. Rolling over onto her back, she struggled to get out of the vest. Then tucked it under her back so the strips wouldn't show.

And heard footsteps, heavy rustling in brush.

She froze, her eyes glued to what she could see through the foliage.

He was getting closer. Oh God. No. *Please not.*

Where the hell was Hawk? Hell, he wouldn't get back for an hour likely.

But she knew if anyone could get here faster, it would be him.

He was good at his job.

So far she'd been good at hers. His voice in her head was even now telling her *stay alive.*

The footsteps walked past. She dared not breathe. With eyes closed, she watched until the footsteps receded. She breathed easier. He was right. She got this.

Until she heard something that made her blood run cold.

"There you are."

Followed by the click of a gun.

She waited but no face appeared.

Loud swearing sounded to the left. She closed her eyes and slid lower.

HAWK GAVE A short terse explanation to the two older men. But he knew their kind from the get go. That old geezer at the wheel had kicked his old truck into high gear and took corners at a speed Hawk didn't think he could. They'd turned that vehicle around and drove him to a different entrance. A small one that he had to crawl into to make his way forward. He'd wanted to go alone, but they weren't having anything to do with it. Especially since this involved Mia.

Now with a brother leading the way and one bringing up the rear, they were motoring. He knew he'd be a few minutes past his said time, but not by much at this pace.

Suddenly Peter came to a stop, his hand out behind him. Hawk came up alongside him and peered into the cavern. From there he could see the entrance where he'd seen the shooter.

Only the damn cavern was empty.

Shit.

He slipped out of the tunnel after giving both men orders to stay behind and raced to the entrance. Flat against the rock wall and cursing himself for leaving Mia alone, he peered into the trees coming up the entrance way. Not a sound. Not a movement.

Damn it. His one advantage was gone. Several large rocks dotted the entrance. He quickly climbed up as high as he could and peered over the top.

There.

He smiled. The killer was walking to every hiding place imaginable and jumped forward as if to freak Mia out. But she hadn't made a sound. He glanced over where he'd left her and frowned. She wasn't there.

"Damn it," the killer snarled. "I don't have time for this."

He walked back toward the cave entrance systematically, shooting into every nook and cranny as if hoping to flush Mia out.

Come closer, Hawk whispered to the killer in his head.

The killer, as if listening to the silent orders, took several steps closer. And came to a stop a few feet away, spun around and roared, "Fuck!"

Hawk jumped him.

The gun went flying. The two men went flying. So did the fists. Hawk managed to get an arm around the asshole's neck and squeezed. The terrorist flipped them both over. And the two men went at it, swearing and sweating with no end in sight.

Just as Hawk swore this asshole had super human strength, the game changed and he found himself struggling to breathe, the killer's hands wrapped around his throat and squeezing the life out of him.

He tried to throw the man off, tried everything he knew to do, but the damn stars were filling his gaze. Shit. He couldn't fail.

And suddenly he was free.

The killer lay flat on the ground beside him, blood running from a gash in his head.

Mia, gasping for breath, held the huge branch she'd armed

herself with earlier. Peter and Paul came flying out of the cave to her side.

Hawk groaned. She threw the club away and dropped to his side and wrapped her arms around his chest, weeping.

He held her close, so damn sure that this time, he'd never get another chance.

Just as he regained his breath and figured that he'd make it once again, a huge truck pulled up beside them. Swede, Shadow, Dane, and damn it, Cooper all hopped out and raced toward them.

CHAPTER 29

M IA SAW DANE race toward her. Swede wasn't far behind. Shadow was in line behind both of them. Tears running down her face, she bolted to her feet and ran straight to him. "He's okay," she cried. "He's fine."

Dane's full on assault slowed as Hawk shifted to a sitting position. To her he looked wonderful, but she knew the men were cataloging the damage to his face and the awkward way he was sitting.

Surrounded by his team, and the brothers who'd joined them from the cave, Hawk explained what happened, adding with great pride in his voice, "Mia belted him up the side of his head with her club."

As all gazes flew to her, she could feel the heat rising on her cheeks, and she shrugged. "He's saved me so many times, it was the least I could do."

"But..." Hawk was once again growling at her. "What did you do wrong?"

She stood over him and snarled right back. "I did nothing wrong. Your job was to save me. My job was to stay alive until you could do that."

He grinned boyishly. "And in this case, you did that perfectly, but what about that, 'Don't move' part," he barked.

She grinned down at him. "I can't make life too easy on you, you know. I have to use my own instinct when the occasion demands it. If I hadn't moved, I'd be dead. He fired shots right into the place where you left me."

With Dane's help, Hawk stood up and opened his arms. "Damn woman will be the death of me."

The men grinned. Dane instantly said, "That's okay. We're all interested, so if you're not keeping her…"

"Back off," he snarled, but there was no heat in his voice. "Besides, maybe she's not interested."

Everyone turned to look at her. She flushed. Talk about a lack of privacy.

"Are you asking if I want to be kept?" she asked cautiously, "'Cause you know my daddy didn't raise me to be a kept woman – right?"

The men guffawed and Hawk's wonderful crooked grin appeared.

"As much as we'd love to hear his explanation for this one," Dane said, "you need to know that when our fearless leader Mason found his perfect mate, we all wanted to keep her for ourselves. Mason finally came to his senses and realized what he'd lose if he didn't make up his mind."

Shadow picked up the story. "Ever since, when we find a girl who might be keeping material, we are of course all interested as we all want what Mason found. Now that Hawk found you and hasn't said if he's keeping you, we're all more than happy to step into his shoes."

Hawk howled, a low level sound erupting from the back of his throat that had the men's grins widening and the poor hapless brothers retreating.

"In the meantime," Swede continued, "we've been asking if he was going to keep you."

"And?" asked Paul curiously, from slightly behind them. "Is he?"

Hawk's howl deepened.

And Mia laughed.

All the men turned to stare at her in surprise as she looked up at Hawk and the frustrated anger on his face.

"What a good question. So Hawk, what's it going to be? Keep me or should I be asking your wonderful team of men who'd like..." they all stepped forward...and she never got a chance to finish.

Hawk's mouth was crushing hers. His lips branded her – not that she needed the reminder as she'd always known where she belonged – she'd just been waiting for him to get the message too...

She was his.

Forever.

This concludes Book 2 of SEALs of Honor: Hawk.

Book 3 is available.

Dane: SEALs of Honor, Book 3

Buy this book at your favorite vendor.

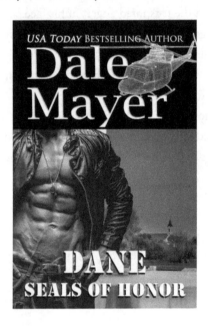

Author's Note

Thank you for reading Hawk: SEALs of Honor, Book 2! If you enjoyed the book, please take a moment and leave a short review.

Dear reader,

I love to hear from readers, and you can contact me at my website: www.dalemayer.com or at my Facebook author page. To be informed of new releases and special offers, sign up for my newsletter. And if you are interested in joining my street team, here is the Facebook sign up page.

Cheers,
Dale Mayer

Touched by Death

Adult RS/thriller

Get this book at your favorite vendor.

Death had touched anthropologist Jade Hansen in Haiti once before, costing her an unborn child and perhaps her very sanity.

A year later, determined to face her own issues, she returns to Haiti with a mortuary team to recover the bodies of an American family from a mass grave. Visiting his brother after the quake, independent contractor Dane Carter puts his life on hold to help the sleepy town of Jacmel rebuild. But he finds it hard to like his brother's pregnant wife or her family. He wants to go home, until he meets Jade – and realizes what's missing in his own life. When the mortuary team begins work, it's as if malevolence has been released from the earth. Instead of laying her ghosts to rest, Jade finds herself confronting death and terror again.

And the man who unexpectedly awakens her heart – is right in the middle of it all.

By Death Series

Touched by Death – Part 1 – FREE
Touched by Death – Part 2
Touched by Death – Parts 1&2
Haunted by Death
Chilled by Death

Vampire in Denial

This is book 1 of the Family Blood Ties Saga

Get this book at your favorite vendor.

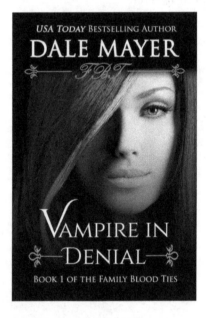

Blood doesn't just make her who she is...it also makes her what she is.

Like being a sixteen-year-old vampire isn't hard enough, Tessa's throwback human genes make her an outcast among her relatives. But try as she might, she can't get a handle on the vampire lifestyle and all the...blood.

Turning her back on the vamp world, she embraces the human teenage lifestyle—high school, peer pressure and finding a boyfriend. Jared manages to stir something in her blood. He's smart and fun and oh, so cute. But Tessa's dream of a having the perfect boyfriend turns into a nightmare when vampires attack the movie theatre and kidnap her date.

Once again, Tessa finds herself torn between the human world and the vampire one. Will blood own out? Can she make peace with who she is as well as what?

Warning: This book ends with a cliffhanger! Book 2 picks up where this book ends.

Family Blood Ties Series

Vampire in Denial – FREE

Vampire in Distress

Vampire in Design

Vampire in Deceit

Vampire in Defiance

Vampire in Conflict

Vampire in Chaos

Vampire in Crisis

Vampire in Control

Family Blood Ties 3in1

Sian's Solution – A Family Blood Ties Short Story

Broken Protocols

Get this book at your favorite vendor.

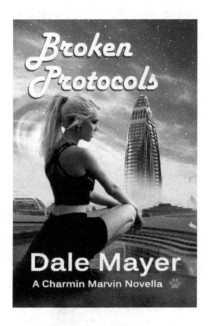

Dani's been through a year of hell...

Just as it's getting better, she's tossed forward through time with her orange Persian cat, Charmin Marvin, clutched in her arms. They're dropped into a few centuries into the future. There's nothing she can do to stop it, and it's impossible to go back.

And then it gets worse...

A year of government regulation is easing, and Levi Blackburn is feeling back in control. If he can keep his reckless brother in check, everything will be perfect. But while he's been protecting Milo from the government, Milo's been busy working on a present for him...

The present is Dani, only she comes with a snarky cat who suddenly starts talking...and doesn't know when to shut up.

In an age where breaking protocols have severe consequences, things go wrong, putting them all in danger...

Charmin Marvin Romantic Comedy Series

Broken Protocols

Broken Protocols 2

Broken Protocols 3

Broken Protocols 3.5

Broken Protocols 1-3

About the Author

Dale Mayer is a USA Today bestselling author best known for her Psychic Visions and Family Blood Ties series. Her contemporary romances are raw and full of passion and emotion (Second Chances, SKIN), her thrillers will keep you guessing (By Death series), and her romantic comedies will keep you giggling (It's a Dog's Life and Charmin Marvin Romantic Comedy series).

She honors the stories that come to her – and some of them are crazy and break all the rules and cross multiple genres!

To go with her fiction, she also writes nonfiction in many different fields with books available on resume writing, companion gardening and the US mortgage system. She has recently published her Career Essentials Series. All her books are available in print and ebook format.

Connect with Dale Mayer Online

Dale's Website – www.dalemayer.com
Twitter – @DaleMayer
Facebook – facebook.com/DaleMayer.author

Also by Dale Mayer

Published Adult Books:

Psychic Vision Series

Tuesday's Child – FREE

Hide'n Go Seek

Maddy's Floor

Garden of Sorrow

Knock, Knock…

Rare Find

Eyes to the Soul

Now You See Her

Psychic Visions 3in1

By Death Series

Touched by Death – Part 1 – FREE

Touched by Death – Part 2

Touched by Death – Parts 1&2

Haunted by Death

Chilled by Death

Second Chances…at Love Series

Second Chances – Part 1 – FREE

Second Chances – Part 2

Second Chances – complete book (Parts 1 & 2)

Charmin Marvin Romantic Comedy Series

Broken Protocols

Broken Protocols 2

Broken Protocols 3

Broken Protocols 3.5

Broken Protocols 1-3

Broken and... Mending

Skin

Scars

Scales (of Justice)

Glory

Genesis

Tori

Celeste

Biker Blues

Biker Blues: Morgan, Part 1

Biker Blues: Morgan, Part 2

Biker Blues: Morgan, Part 3

SEALs of Honor

Mason: SEALs of Honor, Book 1

Hawk: SEALs of Honor, Book 2

Dane: SEALs of Honor, Book 3
Swede: SEALs of Honor, Book 4
Shadow: SEALs of Honor, Book 5
Cooper: SEALs of Honor, Book 6

Collections

Dare to Be You…
Dare to Love…
Dare to be Strong…
RomanceX3

Standalone Novellas

It's a Dog's Life
Riana's Revenge

Published Young Adult Books:

Family Blood Ties Series

Vampire in Denial – FREE
Vampire in Distress
Vampire in Design
Vampire in Deceit
Vampire in Defiance
Vampire in Conflict
Vampire in Chaos
Vampire in Crisis
Vampire in Control
Family Blood Ties 3in1

Sian's Solution – A Family Blood Ties Short Story

Design series
Dangerous Designs – FREE

Deadly Designs

Darkest Designs

Design Series Trilogy

Standalone
In Cassie's Corner

Gem Stone (a Gemma Stone Mystery)

Time Thieves

Published Non-Fiction Books:

Career Essentials
Career Essentials: The Résumé

Career Essentials: The Cover Letter

Career Essentials: The Interview

Career Essentials: 3 in 1